THE
TOYOTOMI
BLADES

Also by Dale Furutani

Death in Little Tokyo

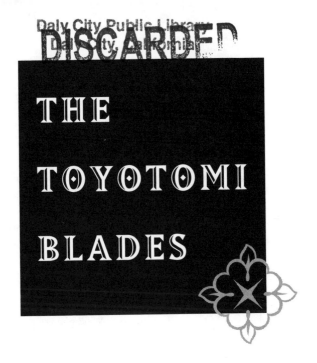

THE TOYOTOMI BLADES

A KEN TANAKA MYSTERY

Dale Furutani

ST. MARTIN'S PRESS
NEW YORK

Design by Ellen R. Sasahara

Library of Congress Cataloging-in-Publication Data

Furutani, Dale.
    The Toyotomi blades : a Ken Tanaka mystery / Dale Furutani.—1st
ed.
        p.   cm.
    ISBN 0-312-17050-5
    I. Title.
PS3556.U778T69   1997
813'.54—dc21   97-20033
                                                            CIP

First Edition: October 1997

10 9 8 7 6 5 4 3 2

To Rose,
a second mother
and an unfailing supporter

Acknowledgments

Special thanks to Shigeki and Eiko Miyamoto and my many friends at Nissan Japan for enjoyable and enlightening trips. Thanks to my *Nihonjin* friends at Nissan U.S.A., Ken Love and the helpful people on the Compuserve Japan Forum who refreshed my memory on obscure details about Japan, Mike Ross for the Torayama *shikona,* Kayko Matsumoto Sonoda and Justice Morio Fukuto for their help, and Marion Spencer for triumphing over my dictation tapes. Finally, I am grateful to Shawn Coyne for buying this series and to Keith Kahla for his editing talents and sage advice.

My footprints on a
Black sand beach. A rising tide
Erases the past.

THE
TOYOTOMI
BLADES

It was a dark and stormy night.

Yeah, yeah, I know the phrase comes from Edward Bulwer-Lytton, who has the dubious distinction of having a bad writing contest named after him. I also know that's how Snoopy starts his one-page novels that never seem to get finished. But darn it, it *was* a dark and stormy night: one of those terrible New York City storms that drives even the muggers and dope dealers off the streets, and at two in the morning it was as dark as a Hollywood producer's heart.

I wasn't there, but he challenged me to figure things out and I've thought about what must have happened countless times. I imagine he started the night by sitting behind the building's parapet, waiting for time to pass and clearing his mind of thoughts of death.

It's a Zen exercise to sit under an icy waterfall and meditate. As you do this, your whole body is transmogrified from shivering flesh to ethereal numbness. Tiny bullets of water impel their way into your consciousness, forcing you to drive into your inner self to remain focused and concentrated. Sitting in the storm that night must have been close to this.

The fierce wind at the top of a fifty-five-story skyscraper would add extra sting to the ice-cold raindrops that assaulted his face and hands. The rest of his body would be clad in garments of tight-fitting black wool that would buffer him from the sting. He knew the rain and the night would make it harder for him to be seen, but it also made the task ahead of him more exacting and much more dangerous.

He must have thought of postponing his task one more night, but the storm had raged for two days, and there was no guarantee that it would clear up soon. He had plane tickets for Europe the next morning and probably he decided not to let the weather deter him or force him to postpone his flight.

From out of the bag he carried to the roof, he took a black woolen hood. He pulled it down over his head, leaving only his eyes and the bridge of his nose exposed. Then he reached into the bag for the rest of his apparatus. It was time to begin.

He strapped a harness onto each foot. The harness held a steel clip that projected downward from the toe. He tied the rest of his gear to one thigh, making sure it wouldn't flop about or make noise, then he picked up the two spring steel tools for his hands. He needed the tools to crawl down the sheer face of the building. He stood up to meet the fury of the storm.

He quickly swung over the top of the parapet and let his legs hang down the front face of the building, dangling high above the surface of the rain-slick street. Below, the street was a black ribbon, with only the blurry headlights of an occasional car visible though the rain. He moved his legs carefully, his toes seeking the thin aluminum frame which marked the separation of the glass panels that formed the front facade of the building. He found it and shoved downwards, wedging the thin steel blades into the rubber stripping that held the glass in the frame.

He stood up, putting his weight on his legs instead of dangling downwards from his arms, then he squatted down, pressing against the glass face of the building. Reaching to the left and to the right with the hand tools, he let the tools bite into the vertical bars holding the glass panels. Pulling inward to support his weight, he lifted one foot, then the other, and hung downwards with his toes searching for the next horizontal strip. When he found it, he released the tension on the vertical frame, shifted his weight to his feet again, and repeated the process. Squatting, hanging by his arms, and extending, slowly making his way down the building like some giant inchworm.

He carefully avoided the windows. The hour was late and most of the residents of the building were asleep, but he still made the necessary detours. He had a long way to go, and he didn't want to be discovered through simple carelessness. His target was eleven stories down, a condominium apartment on the forty-fourth floor.

As he made his way, he didn't feel the rain or the oppressive darkness. Such considerations he held in low regard. His focus was on his mission. After all, he was trained in *Ninjitsu*, the way of the *Ninja*.

When he started his training in Ninjitsu, he was told that a Ninja, if his heart was pure and his technique was perfect, could become invisible if he wanted to; that he could leap thirty-foot castle walls unaided; or, in an echo of the Christian Christ, walk across water. Although he tried earnestly to believe this, he just couldn't surrender doubt about the truth of these claims. Although he was Japanese, his heart held the cynicism of the modern age.

However, he knew from personal experience that, with will and training, a man could do things which others might consider impossible. With the flick of his hand, he could break a glass bottle that was free-standing on a table, shattering the glass without sustaining a cut. In a bitterly cold winter sea, he could hold his breath and glide underwater for impossibly long distances. And, through the use of the cunningly shaped pieces of steel, he could make his way down the blank face of a building.

As he approached his target, he saw a series of brightly lit panels, indicating that the occupant of the apartment was still awake. He stopped right above the lighted rectangles, waiting patiently until it was once again time to act. Just inches below his feet was an apartment window. George LaRusse was standing at this window, looking out into the rain.

The storm is getting worse, LaRusse thought as he took a last drag on his cigarette and crushed it in a full ashtray. In the morning the cleaners would be let into the apartment to put things in order. The poker players had been sent home, some vowing that they would win their money back the next time, and the girls that

LaRusse had called to keep them company had also been dismissed.

There was a time when LaRusse would have asked one or even two of them to stay and spend the night with him, but now he was at an age where sex could be handled in twenty minutes of efficient activity in one of the bedrooms, leaving him more time for the card game and the thrill of winning. Since protection for prostitutes was one of the many businesses he engaged in, LaRusse had become quite jaded about women.

LaRusse walked across the apartment looking at the ashtrays and the dirty drink glasses. The apartment had been decorated for him with modern furniture acting as a counterpoint to the Asian antiques hanging on the walls. The antiques were groups of ancient weapons, samurai swords, a small Chinese shield, and a Chinese spear made of pounded brass, as well as a magnificent gold lacquer screen that covered almost an entire wall of the apartment. The screen was painted with purple iris and green leaves and showed a tranquil pond. LaRusse never felt at home with the decor but wasn't engaged enough to change it. What did interest him was that in the apartment he felt safe.

Due to an unfortunate dispute over territorial rights in a section of Harlem, LaRusse found himself increasingly isolated, wrapped in a glass and steel cocoon and surrounded by bodyguards and tight security. It was beginning to feel like an ornate jail. He walked to a panel on the wall in the hallway and pushed a button. A small TV screen in the panel started to glow, and LaRusse saw a picture of the hallway and elevator outside the front door of his apartment. There, sitting at a desk, was a muscular young man in a conservative business suit.

"Are you going to bed now, Mr. LaRusse?" the man said, speaking into a panel on his desk, where a blue light was glowing.

"Yeah, Fred, it's time for the sack. I'll probably sleep in tomorrow so I won't talk to you before you go off your shift. See you tomorrow night. Good night."

"G'night, Mr. LaRusse," the voice echoed from the wall panel.

LaRusse released his finger from the button and started walking towards his bedroom. On the buffet next to the coffee table he noticed a dish of leftover lasagna.

The lasagna seemed especially good to him tonight. It was sent from his favorite Italian restaurant, Cacciotti's, along with the rest of the food for the poker game. He thought of finishing it off, but he was gaining weight at an alarming rate and had been making half-hearted attempts at dieting. LaRusse decided that he would heat some up in the morning for brunch.

He picked up the dish, took it into the kitchen, and put it in the refrigerator. He thought about pulling out a beer for a nightcap, but decided against it. Making his way to the bedroom, he turned out the lights behind him.

Outside LaRusse's apartment, still clinging to the front of the building, the Ninja saw the lights go out. The man had finally gone to bed. Although it was late, the Ninja knew there were at least four hours of darkness left so he was in no special hurry to go about his business. He would give the man an hour or two to fall asleep before he moved from his position and set about his task.

A couple of hours later, LaRusse awoke groggy and sleepy-eyed. He had to go to the bathroom. He climbed his way out of sleep and into consciousness, and just as he reached the state that balanced between being asleep and being awake, he heard a small sound. He couldn't tell if he actually heard it or dreamed it, but he reached under his pillow and placed his hand on the gun he kept there. He operated on instinct, and instinct had kept him alive in many tight situations. He stayed still, fighting his way to full alertness, listening.

The sound puzzled him. It was the noise of wind, but too loud to be coming from outside his apartment. The location of the sound also puzzled him. It came from his living room, and sounds of people breaking in should come from the hall. Keeping one hand on the gun, he reached with his other hand to the intercom by his bed.

"Fred?" LaRusse's voice was a hoarse whisper as he called the guard's name.

"Yes, sir?" The intercom's volume was turned low, but the puzzled surprise in the guard's voice still came through.

"Everything okay?"

"Yes, sir. Quiet night. Nothin' going on. Is something the matter?"

"No," LaRusse said after a pause. "Just thought I'd check to make sure you were awake. Good night."

"G'night, sir."

LaRusse clicked off the intercom. He lay in bed puzzling out the mystery of the sound. He was forty-four stories above the street and there was only one door to the apartment. He felt the stir of a cool draft and he decided that the sound must be from the heating system. It was always acting up. He took his hand off the gun and threw back the covers, finally getting up to go to the bathroom.

On the way back to bed, he thought about the dish of lasagna; he could taste the aromatic tomato sauce, firm noodles, seasoned meat, and the creamy cheese. To hell with his diet. He was hungry and he wanted that lasagna. He padded back out of the bedroom and down the hall.

The apartment definitely felt colder than normal, and when he entered the living room on his way to the kitchen, he was astounded to smell rain and to feel the chill of the storm. Before him, an entire panel of glass was removed and lying on the living room floor. The wind and rain were beating in through the windowless opening, causing a widening stain on the expensive carpet.

His first thought was that the storm must have somehow worked the glass free, popping it out of its frame. He walked over to investigate and noticed that there was some kind of suction cup clamped to the face of the glass. The suction cup had been used to remove the glass.

LaRusse turned immediately to retrieve his gun, but before his turn was complete, a knife flew across the room with power and authority. It penetrated the flesh just below his right jaw. The suddenness of the attack and the massive drop in blood pressure from the severing of an artery muted the pain and fear, leaving him confused more than anything else. As he tried to pull the knife from his flesh, he staggered, stepped on the slippery wet pane of glass, and fell backwards through the opening.

As he started the long tumble to the street, the confusion cleared and the cold ratiocination that he had depended on for his livelihood and life returned. His senses became acutely aware of everything that was happening. He felt the warm gush of blood on his hands as he continued to try to remove the knife. He felt the sharp sting of the blade as he tugged at it. He felt the lesser sting of the drops of cold water hitting him on the face, hands, and bare feet. He saw the blur of glass panels passing him as he tumbled towards the earth, and he noted with detachment that he continued to pick up speed.

Perversely, his last thoughts were of the hunger he still felt and how the lasagna in his refrigerator was so much better than his mother's.

The Ninja hesitated only long enough to make sure the man wasn't going to be a threat. The need to press his attack was eliminated when the man fell through the window opening. He was surprised at how little time it took to actually kill a man. It was his first.

He had wanted to avoid a confrontation with the owner of the apartment, but hadn't shrunk from the necessity of acting. It was just like his practice. Over and over, endless repetitions of throwing a knife. That repetition was how he had acquired the skills that made up his *gei,* or art. To him it was an art, and the death of the man was the natural extension of that art, an extension that turned his years of rather esoteric training into a practical craft. The craft of killing.

He turned his attention back to the wall of the living room where the real target of his efforts was hanging.

2

Two days later, the cold wind of Rotterdam was dancing around the cars on Oude Binnenweg as the silver-and-white tourist bus pulled to the curb and shuddered to a halt.

"Gentlemen, we come to the next stop." Wouter Leeuwenberg's English was slightly accented but his meaning was clear. There were groans and considerable conversation when the group saw they were parked in front of another museum. Since the conversation was in Japanese and Leeuwenberg spoke no Japanese, he couldn't understand what they were saying. But he could guess.

The common language between Leeuwenberg and the Japanese tour group was English so he felt safe speaking to the bus driver in Dutch. "Oh-oh, the natives are getting restless."

"What are you going to do?" the driver asked.

"What can I do? That horse's ass Hans scheduled us for six museums today. Six! This is the fourth and even I'm getting sick of it. These guys have already seen the palaces of London, the art of Paris, and the sex shops of Copenhagen. Then I get them." He groaned. "I'll show them Rotterdam, but why does Hans put together an itinerary that starts with six museums on the first day?"

The last of the tourists filed out of the bus and Leeuwenberg started after them. "I think Hans hates me," he called over his shoulder to the bus driver as he stepped out after them.

One of the Japanese tourists approached him. He had chubby

cheeks and a smooth face that made him look like he was twelve years old. "Excuse me, but what is this museum?" he asked.

Leeuwenberg smiled his best tour guide smile and said, "This is the Hollandse Scheepvaart. Very famous! Major attraction!"

The Japanese had a look of skepticism cross his face that approached incredulity. He said something to the rest of the group and a lot of disgusted muttering in Japanese passed between the members of the tour. Then he said something and the group laughed.

He turned back to Leeuwenberg. "This is a famous museum?"

"Yes, it is," Leeuwenberg lied.

"Ah," the Japanese answered. "The Louvre!"

"No, not the Louvre. The Louvre is in Paris. This is the Hollandse Scheepvaart. The Dutch Shipping Museum."

"But this is a famous museum?"

"Yes."

"Ah, the British Museum!"

"No, it's not the British Museum! It's the Hollandse . . ." Leeuwenberg's heated correction died as he noticed the twinkle in his questioner's eye and the laughter from the rest of the group. So much for the inscrutable Japanese, Leeuwenberg thought, as he bustled past to lead the group out of the wind and into the museum. He was going to have a mutiny on his hands if he didn't get this tour going right away.

Inside the museum, another Japanese face wasn't so openly mirroring his thoughts. As the only Asian face in the sparsely populated museum, he knew he would be conspicuous. And he had built his career on not being conspicuous.

He knew that Japanese tour groups were taken through on a regular basis, so he had delayed his inspection until such a group showed up. The flock of Japanese businessmen headed by a bustling Leeuwenberg entered the museum, and the man studied the group carefully. He decided that it would do. In this group of tourists, he could disappear as surely as he could on a darkened night.

He approached the stragglers at the end of the group and asked if they would mind if he followed them through the museum. A few members of the group thought this request unusual and perhaps even a bit impolite, but they didn't dream of refusing a fellow countryman.

As he walked through the museum with the group, the man loosened his tie and mimicked the reluctant shuffle of the businessmen, even though he was anxious to see something. Like a chameleon, he adapted to his surroundings and blended in so effectively that Leeuwenberg didn't notice that his tour group had increased by one. The man showed patience as Leeuwenberg took them by dingy ship models and exhibits that celebrated Holland's past as a major maritime power. The only thing that raised even a flicker of interest in him was a model of Henry Hudson's ship, *The Half Moon,* which the guide said was used to discover the Hudson River. The man had been in New York only a few days before.

His patience was rewarded when the group went into a section of the museum devoted to the Dutch presence in Nagasaki. In the 1600s the Dutch had a monopoly on access to Japan through a community in the port of Nagasaki. The museum had maps and artifacts depicting this community, including a model of the tiny island to which the Dutch community was confined. The island, made artificially rectangular by stone sea walls, was linked to the mainland by a single bridge. There was a guard tower at the mainland side that made the Dutch enclave look like what it was designed to be: a prison that would keep the corrupting European influence away from the people. In the five minutes the group spent at the exhibit, the man absorbed every detail, committing the placement of doors, windows, and cabinets to memory.

When the tour group returned to the museum lobby, Leeuwenberg meticulously counted them. He had the exact number he started with, and he had no hint that he had hosted an additional member during the tour. A few of the Japanese near the back of the group noticed that the stranger was missing, but none knew exactly when he had disappeared. Any lingering curiosity about the man vanished when Leeuwenberg suggested, "Would you gentlemen care to delete two museums from today's tour and visit some Rotterdam cabarets? You can drink Dutch beer." A ragged cheer of enthusiasm rose as Leeuwenberg's statement was translated into Japanese and passed on.

Two hours later, the museum went through its normal closing routine. Two guards walked through the various rooms asking a few lingering members of the public to leave. One of the guards walked into the men's room, looking under the stall doorways to see if he could see any shoes. Seeing nothing, he turned off the light and exited the men's room, continuing his rounds.

The man was crouched on top of the toilet seat in a back stall. A schoolboy's trick, but sometimes the simplest strategies are the best. He waited.

A few hours later, the door of the restroom opened. The man carefully looked down the darkened hall. There was no evidence of life. During his tour of the museum, the man had carefully noted there were no key boxes, which indicated there was no night watchman, so he was fairly confident he would not be disturbed. He stepped into the hallway and made his way towards the Nagasaki exhibit.

The object he was looking for was in a glass case near the model of the Dutch settlement. He pulled out a collection of lock picks and inserted one pick into the cabinet lock to make an exploratory probe. It was a simple lock and he felt the tumblers turn under a little pressure from the face of the pick. He wiggled the pick around, twisted, and the lock snapped open. He lifted the top of the glass case, reached inside, and took his prize. Then he relocked the case.

He walked to a window he had previously chosen. Reaching into his pocket, he pulled out a scrap of wire. He carefully wrapped the ends of the bare wire around the contacts for the alarm sensor guarding the window, shorting out the sensor and making it possible for him to open the window without setting off the alarm.

He took out a small flashlight and risked shining the light for a few seconds to make sure the wire was connected to the proper contacts. Then, on a whim, he extracted a length of string from another pocket and securely tied it to the wire that was shorting out the alarm system. When he was satisfied with the connections, he unlocked and opened the window. The alarm stayed silent.

He climbed through the window into an alley running behind the museum. He ran the string tied to the shorting wire outside with him and closed the window until it was almost fully shut. Then he tugged at the string until the shorting wire was worked off the alarm contacts and pulled outside through the narrow opening of the window. He shut the window the last fraction of an inch and used a flat piece of metal to poke up between the two parts of the window and swing the lock back in place. The man allowed himself a grin as he put the metal, wire, and string in his pocket. When the authorities discovered the theft, the locked cabinet and untripped alarm would give them something to puzzle over.

Looking both ways, he put the stolen object in a long brown paper sack and stuck it under his arm like a loaf of French bread. Nonchalantly, he walked out of the alley towards his rented car parked a few blocks away. He whistled a little tune as he walked, happy as any tourist.

A few hours later another man was whistling, but this time it was literally half a world away, in Tokyo, Japan. His whistling was an absentminded habit when his thoughts were absorbed by a problem. He was a tall man, wearing a wrinkled gray suit over a white knit shirt that was yellowed from neglect. His hair was closely cropped to his head and his skin was pockmarked. He walked towards the California Orange bar with a long loping gait, much like a wolf.

The bar was in the Shinjuku district of Tokyo, and when he entered, it took a few seconds to let his eyes adjust to the dim lighting. The bar catered to students, and at thirty-eight, he was easily the oldest person in the establishment. Even the bartender looked young.

The walls were decorated with broad slashes of color and a long bar dominated the narrow room. It was early afternoon, but there were a dozen young people populating the room, mostly sitting in groups of three or four. The music coming over the sound system was a Japanese rap song and the older man curled his lip.

Lately, four out of five top hits in Japan were rap songs, and the surrender to percussive cacophony offended him. He much preferred the traditional and melodic Japanese *enka* music.

Sitting at the bar was the person he was looking for, nineteen-year-old Yasuo Ishibashi. The young man was nursing a beer, and he seemed to be sitting at the far end of the bar to avoid company. Ishibashi looked troubled, and his gaze was focused on his beer mug.

The older man strode over to the open stool next to Ishibashi and sat down. Ishibashi looked up briefly, and morosely returned to staring at his beer. When the older man caught the bartender's attention, he ordered a Johnnie Walker Black Label, an expensive drink in Tokyo. When the drink was served, he sipped it and smacked his lips in appreciation. Then he started talking to Ishibashi. "Do you come here often?"

Ishibashi looked offended that his solitude had been disturbed, but politeness forced him to answer. "Pretty often."

Given a wedge, the older man continued, "Are you a student?"

"Waseda," Ishibashi said, naming an expensive private university.

"Waseda!" the older man said. "My brother went to Waseda. I'm a great admirer of your school." The man gave Ishibashi a toothy grin, revealing a row of badly aligned teeth highlighted by a prominent gold front tooth.

Ishibashi gave the rumpled man next to him a surprised look. The thought of any relative of this disheveled character going to Waseda seemed to startle him. Before Ishibashi could say anything, the man offered, "Let me buy you a drink."

"No, thank you. That's very nice of you, but you don't have to buy me a drink."

"Nonsense!" the older man insisted. He waved at the bartender, who came over to the end of the bar. "Bring my young friend a drink," the older man said. "Do you like Johnnie Walker or Chivas?" he asked Ishibashi.

Nonplussed, Ishibashi said, "Johnnie Walker is fine, thank you, but you don't have to buy me a drink."

"Nothing is too good for a Waseda student," the older man said. "You're the future hope of our country."

Ishibashi waved his hand as if to brush off both the compliment and the drink, but the bartender was already pouring. Sighing, he picked up the drink and poured it down. Johnnie Walker Black, which was far above his drinking budget, did taste good. Before he could finish the first drink, the weird fellow next to him was already waving for another round.

A few hours later, the older man was checking into one of Tokyo's many love motels. In a land famed for its scarcity of space and privacy, love motels exist to provide amorous couples with both, at any time of the day or night. No desk clerk handled the check-in, because all transactions at this motel were handled discreetly by credit card and computer, with no humans to interfere with anonymity and secrecy.

The man inserted a recently stolen credit card into the check-in machine, and a video monitor flashed a polite greeting in *kanji* on its screen and directed him to room 116 with a little map. A magnetically encoded key was extended from a slot, and as he took the key, an admonition appeared on the screen reminding him to return the key when he was done because the room was being charged to the credit card by the hour.

The man returned briefly to the underground parking lot that served the motel. He looked around to assure himself that he was still alone before he opened the door to his Toyota. Sleeping soundly on the back seat was Ishibashi, drunk and snoring loudly. The man reached into the back of the car and took out a small bag. Then he rousted the sleeping student and helped him out of the car. With the drunk Ishibashi leaning against his shoulder and weaving unsteadily, the man and the youth made their way to room 116.

The magnetic key unlatched the door and they entered the room. The windowless room contained a bed covered with a garish red cover, a television, two doors along one wall, and an enormous mirror mounted on another wall to reflect any activity on the bed. The man dumped Ishibashi on the bed and chained the door behind them.

Placing the bag on the floor he walked over to the doors on the opposite wall and opened one. It was a toilet. He closed the door and opened the second door. It was a Japanese-style bathroom with a large heart-shaped tub. The room had a drain in the tile floor, low-set faucets on the wall, and two small stools. He took one of the stools out of the bathroom and positioned it by the bed.

He then perched on the edge of the bed and looked at the youth for a few moments, contemplating his next actions. While he sat there he noticed the sounds of a couple in the next room coming through the too-thin walls. They were moaning and groaning and occasionally the woman was shouting terms of endearment in both Japanese and French. He couldn't decide if it was an office lady who thought speaking French during lovemaking was sexy, or a hooker who was entertaining a visiting French tourist. Either way, the woman speaking French during sex seemed to symbolize everything he hated about what Japan had become. Her voice spoiled what he had come for.

He turned on the TV, twisting the sound knob savagely to maximum volume. Before the picture came on there was a notice on the screen that the television would be an extra charge to the credit card. When the notice disappeared, the screen dissolved into a soft-core Japanese porno film showing a scene with a young girl running naked on a beach. Because Japanese censors don't allow frontal nudity, a blue dot floated on the screen to cover her crotch. He wasn't interested in the girl, but he was grateful that the booming music that accompanied the girl's capering on the beach drowned out the sounds from the next room.

He turned his attention to his bag and unzipped the top. He took a length of rope from the bag. He placed the bathroom stool directly under the light fixture in the room's ceiling and stood on the stool. Reaching up, he was able to tie the rope around the fixture. He stepped off the stool and went over to Ishibashi. The young man had fallen into a drunken stupor again, and a line of drool was dripping down his face.

The older man roused Ishibashi and got him off the bed. He led him over to the stool and tried to hoist the drunken youth onto the stool.

"What're you doing?" the young man asked.

"Just cooperate for a moment," the older man said.

"Cooperate?"

"Don't you want to end your troubles? I have a way for you to do it."

"What do you know about my troubles?" the youth mumbled.

"I know all about them and I've decided to help you out of them."

"What do you mean?"

"I'll explain in a minute. For now, just cooperate and stand on the stool."

The youth was clearly puzzled, but in his drunken state he couldn't fathom what was happening and docilely did as he was asked to.

"What are you doing?" Ishibashi protested as the older man tied the rope around his neck. As the young man raised his hands to his neck to remove the rope, the older man quickly kicked the stool away.

When Ishibashi's weight hit the rope, the light fixture gave way and partially pulled out of the ceiling. This was a development the older man had not planned for. He had expected Ishibashi's neck to snap, but instead, with the failed light fixture absorbing some of the shock, Ishibashi was hanging from the rope by his neck with his feet barely brushing the floor.

Tremendous pain shot through the young man's body, sobering him up as the rope jerked at his neck, crushing his windpipe. In the large mirror Ishibashi could see himself dangling from the rope with the half-pulled-out light fixture above. His toes skimmed the floor, but he wasn't low enough to relieve the pressure on his neck by standing on his tiptoes. He reached out to the older man standing next to him, trying to grab him for support. The older man stepped back.

Ishibashi clawed at the rope and tried to pull himself up to release the pain and tension from his neck. He was partially successful and tried to croak out a yell for help. From his crushed larynx a hoarse sound emerged and the effort caused him even more pain. Hanging from his neck and hands, Ishibashi tried to ignore the new pain and continued to shout. His feeble shouting made no impression on the older man or the couple in the next room. Even if the couple could be distracted from their passion, the loud sound of the television drowned out Ishibashi's weakening croaks for help.

Gradually, while watching himself strangle in the big mirror on the opposite wall, Ishibashi felt himself succumbing to pain and weakness. His strength gave out and he could no longer suspend himself hanging from the rope. The noose tightened. His toes frantically scratched at the surface of the carpeting in the room trying to support his weight. It was incomprehensible to Ishibashi that the older man had done this to him. He had just met him in the bar. He tried to curse the man, but the rope was too tight around his neck and he could only make a weak gurgling noise. Finally, Ishibashi lost bodily control before slipping into unconsciousness and death.

When the older man was sure the youth was dead, he briefly thought about retying the rope to hoist the body higher. But the growing brown stain on the young man's pants made the older man reluctant to make a neat job of the faked suicide. He wrinkled his nose at the smell and decided he didn't want to do more.

"If you were a tough guy, you wouldn't be here," the older man said with contempt to the dangling body. In Japanese slang a tough guy is someone who can hold his liquor. The older man inspected the room, wiping down doorknobs and the stool with a handkerchief to get rid of fingerprints. Then, after turning down the volume on the TV while using the handkerchief as a glove, he quietly left.

While things that would directly affect my life were happening literally around the world, I was sitting in Los Angeles feeling fat, dumb, and happy.

Well, I guess fat isn't totally accurate, although I do have that extra five to ten pounds that seem to attach themselves to your body around your fortieth birthday. Dumb isn't totally accurate either, although I felt pretty dumb when I lost my computer programming job as part of what is euphemistically known as corporate downsizing. I felt dumb about devoting countless hours to a corporation that was willing to cut hundreds of employee jobs without cutting a single executive. But despite the weight and the lack of a job, happy was a totally accurate description.

I was sitting in the living room of my apartment in the Silver Lake section of Los Angeles sharing good news with my girlfriend, Mariko Kosaka. I held up a letter that had been delivered by DHL, the next-day overseas courier service, and asked Mariko, "Do you want me to read it to you?"

"Of course, Ken. You dragged me down here just so you could read it, so don't play coy with me now," Mariko answered.

With a sheepish grin, I looked at the letter and started reading.

"Dear Mr. Tanaka. I am the foreign guest booking producer for the Japanese television program News

Pop. News Pop *is a blend of current news stories and live interviews, and it's very popular in Japan. We noted with interest your participation in solving the murder of Mr. Matsuda, as reported in the* Asahi Shimbun *newspaper. We feel this story would also be of interest to our viewers and we would like you to appear on our television show either next weekend or the weekend following. We realize this is short notice, but I'm sure you can appreciate that our program likes to present stories while they are still topical and in the public's mind. If you can appear on either show, please contact me by fax or at the number listed on our letterhead. If you would like, please feel free to reverse the telephone charges. If you can appear on the program, we will pay your airfare to Japan and food and lodging expenses for a period of up to five days. You will stay at the luxurious Imperial Hotel in Tokyo and fly business class to Japan via ANA. I hope you will be able to accept our invitation, and I look forward to hearing from you at your earliest possible convenience. Yours truly, Buzz Sugimoto, Foreign Guest Booking Producer.*"

I looked at Mariko. "Well, what do you think?"

"What kind of Japanese name is Buzz?"

I sighed. "I don't care if his name is Alphonse. Weren't you listening? They're offering me a free trip to Japan and a chance to be on Japanese television."

"I was listening quite carefully and I noticed the offer was only for you. It should have been for you and your incredibly glamorous actress girlfriend."

"You're just jealous."

"Damn right I'm jealous. It sounds like a fabulous invitation and I'm going to be envious of every glorious moment you're going to have on this trip."

"Why don't you join me?"

Mariko held up her hand and rubbed her thumb and forefinger together. "I'm broke. You should know that's a natural state for a struggling actress. Your trip is free, but mine would cost a fortune."

"When I call them I could ask them if they'd pay for your trip, too."

"Don't be crazy. This is a great deal and you shouldn't screw it up. Besides, I like the idea of you getting more recognition for solving Matsuda's murder. It got just a small piece in the L.A. *Times*. I was glad the *Rafu Shimpo* and *Tozai Times* picked up the story, and even more gratified when the papers in Japan picked it up."

After I solved the murder of a Japanese businessman in a Los Angeles hotel, Mariko was my biggest booster. Most of the press coverage I got was due to her efforts. She hunted down any press mention of the case and contacted the Los Angeles Japanese language newspapers, the *Rafu Shimpo* and *Tozai Times,* urging them to feature the story, which they did. From these stories, I was interviewed by Los Angeles–based reporters for several Japanese newspapers, including the *Asahi Shimbun,* which is Japan's largest newspaper.

In the *Asahi Shimbun,* I got a full-page feature story that included a nice picture of me holding a Japanese samurai sword. The businessman was killed with a sword, and when the reporter and photographer showed up at my apartment for the interview, the photographer spotted a newly acquired samurai sword that I had hanging on my apartment wall. The photographer had me hold the sword as a prop. Neither Mariko nor I speak or read Japanese, but she hunted down a half-dozen copies of the newspaper with my picture in it at Los Angeles' Kinokuniya Bookstore. I told her that if she put half the effort into promoting herself that she put into promoting my amateur crime solving, she'd be the best-known actress since Ingrid Bergman. Her response was "If it was only that easy."

"What's the harm if I ask them to pay for you to come along, too?" I asked.

"Ken, this is your fifteen minutes of fame, even if it does seem to be mostly in Japanese. Don't blow it. Enjoy it. After I become an enormously successful actress, I can act snotty for the both of us. But for now, take the free trip and just know that I'm not only jealous as hell about this, I'm also enormously proud of you."

How can you return to a place you've never been? That's something I puzzled over as I pressed my face against the hazy Plexiglas of the plane window. Through my cheek I could feel the cold of forty-eight thousand feet.

I was flying in the upper cabin of a 747 and loving it. I've flown on Boeing 747s before, but I didn't realize that some of them have an upper deck with about twenty business class seats. On domestic flights, I've always flown in what airlines call economy class, but which I call steerage. On a 747, steerage means a lot of people jammed into a confined space. In the upper deck the seats were only two abreast and there were two flight attendants to take care of our needs. When I boarded the plane and climbed the spiral staircase that went to the upper deck, I noticed the plush leather-covered seats for first class in the front of the plane, but I wasn't envious. On my only other international flight, I was jammed in a MATS plane with more than one hundred other teenagers going to war in Vietnam, all of us trying not to show how scared we were. Business class to Japan was my best flying experience. If that makes me a bumpkin, then I plead guilty.

Below, on the horizon, came the coast of Japan. All I could see was a thin, gray line that might or might not turn into something more interesting as the plane rushed forward. I was disappointed that the coastline didn't provide a more spectacular view. Although I've never been to Japan, I felt that in some way this was a homecoming. I've always considered Hawaii home, even though I've now lived in Los Angeles for most of my life. My family's been in Hawaii since 1896, but my grandfather and grandmother came from Japan. So, although Hawaii is home, Japan is the homeland.

I'm a *Sansei,* or third generation Japanese-American. Like most third generation Americans, I've forgotten a lot of my roots, but I'm still aware of all sorts of influences on my outlook and actions that are caused by the fact that my grandparents were Japanese. Certainly the way I fit into American society has been affected because of that heritage.

The airplane's public address system came to life and something was said in Japanese. I was flying All Nippon Airlines, ANA, and it made me vaguely uncomfortable that all announcements were first made in Japanese and then English. In case of an emergency, I didn't want every Japanese-speaking passenger up and rushing for an exit while I was still waiting for a translation.

"Ladies and gentlemen," the voice on the PA finally began in English, "we will be landing at Narita in approximately fifty minutes, so if you have not already done so, please fill out your disembarkation pass for submission to Japanese customs."

I checked the small white card that all visitors have to fill out and put it back in my pocket. I took a few deep breaths. At Los Angeles International Airport, I had been surprisingly nervous, and sensing my mood, Mariko had given me an especially loving send-off. I don't know what I was nervous about, but I think it was a combination of going to Japan for the first time and the prospect of being on television. Like any Angeleno, I'm pretty blasé about the entertainment business because there's so much of it in the city. But this would be my first time on television, and to complicate things, it would be a live show and in Japanese.

To pass the time, I took a copy of *Things Very, Very Japanese* by Bob Thomas from my travel bag. I sought the card I had stuck in as a bookmark and started reading a piece on *tsuba,* Japanese decorative sword guards. I bought three guidebooks for my trip to Japan. Books on Japan are like books about sex or music—they explain things in academic terms, but they can't convey the feelings or emotions involved in the actual experience.

I know a lot of individual Japanese words and phrases, and in college I studied Japanese history. Despite that, I never visited the object of my interest. In Yasunari Kawabata's novel *Snow Country* there's a character who's an expert on Western ballet. In spite of having an encyclopedic knowledge on the subject, he has never actually seen a ballet. In some ways, I emulate this character.

A few minutes later, I looked out the window again and the gray line on the horizon had turned into a rocky coastline. The plane was too high to make out details, but I could see how rugged and mountainous the land was. As the plane came lower in its approach to Tokyo International Airport at Narita, I saw fall colors breaking through the haze. Red, yellow, and a pale orange splashed the trees that were clustered on the mountainsides. Spoiling the beauty, I also saw that great gouges had been taken out of some of the hills, exposing raw, red earth. The mountains were also crisscrossed with ugly electrical lines and high-tension towers. The woods, towers, and gouges formed a crazy quilt that didn't match my notions of how ordered Japan would be.

Once I arrived at the airport, my idea of Japanese efficiency was reaffirmed. The airport was crowded, but clean and well run to the point of coldness. At the immigration desk, the clerk looked at my American passport and silently looked up to confirm that the owner matched the picture.

I took one of the metal carts provided and gathered up my luggage as it appeared on the endless belt. I then joined the mass of Japanese and tourists lining up for customs inspection. I moved the cart to one of the customs stations with the green nonresident sign. When it was my turn to have my baggage inspected, the Japanese customs agent in the gray-blue uniform glared at me. In L.A. gang terms, he gave me a hard look. In Hawaii, we'd call it the stink eye. Whatever you call it, it was plain he wasn't happy. He said something in Japanese. I gave the agent a puzzled look. The agent repeated himself, this time much more harshly.

"Excuse me, but do you speak English? I'm afraid I don't speak Japanese," I said.

The agent looked at me in surprise. "Are you an American?" he asked in very good English.

It never occurred to me that I would be taken for a Japanese national, although obviously, with two Japanese-American parents, I look Japanese. "Yes, I am," I said.

His whole demeanor changed. A smile spread across his face and he pulled my bags through the customs table without checking a single one. "Welcome to Japan," the agent said cheerily.

I walked out of the baggage area into a milling mass of people. Most appeared to be families looking for loved ones, but a great number were limousine drivers or businessmen holding signs with names in English or Japanese. When I'd called Sugimoto to set up the trip, he'd said he'd meet me at the airport, so I scanned the businessmen to see if I could spot one holding a sign with my name on it. As I was searching for Sugimoto, a man came up to me. He was dressed in a plain white T-shirt, Levi's jeans, black motorcycle boots, and a black leather belt with a large, silver Harley-Davidson belt buckle. His hair looked permed into curls and he wore it with an authentic 1950s jelly-roll lock of hair cascading down his forehead.

In the Thomas book about Japan I had read about the youngsters who gather at Yoyogi Park every Sunday all decked out in 1950s American regalia, complete with black leather jackets and poodle skirts. The young people go there to dance, play music, and meet other kids. Those kids were teenagers, but this man was at least in his midthirties, and he seemed long-of-tooth for dressing up like James Dean. To my surprise, he stuck out his hand and said, "Mr. Tanaka, I'm Buzz Sugimoto."

He must have been used to people doing double takes, because he showed no reaction when I did mine. This kind of appearance could be expected in Los Angeles, but here in Tokyo it was totally incongruous to me. I had enough wit to shake his hand.

"I recognize you from the picture," Sugimoto added in slightly accented English, "or else I'd be holding up one of the little cardboard signs with your name on it. Is that all your luggage? I have a car waiting outside."

Sugimoto took over my luggage cart and wheeled it out of the terminal with me in tow. Outside, there was a black limousine waiting at the curb. The driver was in a blue uniform, wearing white cotton gloves. He had a feather duster in his hand and he seemed busy dusting off the car. The car was a Nissan President, a model they don't sell in the States. Sugimoto spoke to the driver in Japanese and opened the door of the limo for me. "The driver will take care of your luggage," Sugimoto said as I climbed into the car. The seats of the car had white lace doilies pinned to the headrests. It looked very Victorian.

"How long will it take us to get to the hotel?" I asked Sugimoto.

"It's rush hour now. It will take us at least two hours, maybe longer. If you don't mind, I'd like to stop at the studio before we check you into the hotel. We'd like to film a short promotional spot with you for next week's show."

The news that it might take over two hours to get to Tokyo made me wish that I'd used a bathroom before leaving the terminal, but the driver was already in the car and pulling away from the curb before I could say anything.

It was late afternoon Japan time, which made it very late at night in Los Angeles, and my body was still on Los Angeles time. The thought of stopping at a studio to film some promo was not as inviting as the thought of checking into the hotel and sleeping. Still, I figured it would be churlish not to let *News Pop* make its promotional piece. After all, they had flown me to Japan to be on the show, not for my sparkling personality. I told Sugimoto that stopping at the studio would be fine.

"Did you bring the sword?" Sugimoto asked.

"Yes. It's in that large gym bag."

"And that's the sword used in the murder you solved?"

"No," I said, surprised. "The murder sword is a piece of evidence, so it's being held by the Los Angeles Police Department. This sword is one that I bought for a hundred dollars at a garage sale."

"It's not the murder sword? When we saw the photograph we naturally assumed that the sword you were holding was the one used in the murder."

"I'm afraid not. It's just a prop that the *Asahi Shimbun* photographer thought would add interest to the picture."

"Damn!" Sugimoto thought a few seconds, and said more to himself than to me, "Never mind. If we made a mistake thinking it was the murder sword, others might make the same mistake. We'll still use it as a prop in the promotional piece. Have you ever been on television before?"

"No, I haven't."

"Well, don't worry. Our show has live interviews, but we do interviews with people who aren't professionals all the time. During the interview we'll run a simultaneous translation from Japanese to English through an earpiece, so you'll understand the questions that our hosts ask you. You'll respond in English, naturally, and we'll do a simultaneous translation for our audience. Prior to the live interview we'll discuss the types of questions we'll ask you, so although your responses will be spontaneous, there will be no surprises. The lead-in piece, which sets up the interview, will be on tape. We'll need your help in putting together that piece, so we'd like you to check in at the studio for about an hour every day. The late afternoon is best, which will also give you most of the day for sightseeing. Do you have any questions?"

"No. You must give that little speech a great many times," I said.

Sugimoto laughed. "I'm sorry if I sound a little like a recording. I do give that speech a lot."

"Do you meet many people at the airport?"

"Quite a few. It's part of my job when I'm in town. Half the time, I'm traveling to the U.S. or Europe to track down stories. In fact, I just got back from Europe a few days ago. I'm not always here to meet our guests, but it's actually something I enjoy because I get to know a great many people."

"How long have you been doing this kind of work?"

"About seven years. I've been doing it for *News Pop* for three years. Before that I worked with other shows, including *NHK News*."

We made small talk as we drove along, but my attention soon turned to the view out the car window during the long drive from Narita to Tokyo. I saw a lot of roofs made with blue tile or tin sheets, and the houses were very small and narrow even when they were built near Narita, where there seemed to be more open space. Small houses crowded together is hardly an original observation about Japan, but when you see it for yourself you realize that many facets of the Japanese standard of living simply haven't kept up with their vaunted technical and business prowess.

Traffic increased as we approached Tokyo. Sugimoto pointed out Tokyo Disneyland off the freeway and said we had at least another hour to go, but frankly, by that time, my thoughts were more focused on my bladder than the Japanese version of a Southern California tourist attraction. I really should have gone to the bathroom before we left the airport.

5

We crawled through bumper-to-bumper traffic. There seemed to be no lane discipline with Tokyo drivers, and cars were often five abreast where there were just three lanes painted on the pavement. In Japan, of course, they drive on the left side of the road like the British, and it was a little disorienting to see drivers on the "wrong" side.

It took us almost two and a half hours to reach the television studio from Narita, and when we finally got there I was desperate. We pulled up to what looked like a side entrance to the studio and when we got out of the car, Sugimoto asked me to take the prop sword out. Instead, I told Sugimoto, "I have to use a restroom. Now. Right away. Immediately."

"No problem," Sugimoto said, and led me to a small bathroom off the entrance. As soon as I walked into the bathroom, I knew there actually was a problem.

In the room there was no toilet and no urinal. There was a sink and in the tile floor there was a fixture that baffled me. It looked like a white porcelain version of the kind of slit trenches we used for field latrines in the army, but with a raised lip at one end. It was about eight inches wide and two feet long. I stared at it for several minutes trying to figure out what the hell it was.

Embarrassed but in need of immediate guidance, I stuck my head out of the door and asked Sugimoto, "How are you supposed to use this thing?"

Sugimoto laughed and said, "That depends on what you want to do. Why don't I take you to a Western-style toilet? Sometimes the Japanese-style toilets can be confusing."

"I'm not totally confused, but I do want to know if what I'm about to do is the right thing. I thought I'd just straddle that trench in the floor and take careful aim. Is that right?"

"You got it," Sugimoto said.

I went back into the toilet and did a reasonably neat job. When I finished I stared at the fixture in the floor, trying to fathom how you would use it if you needed it for other bodily functions or if you were a woman. The possibilities I came up with all involved straddling, squatting, and other undignified maneuvers. I had just received my first prosaic lesson in the differences between the familiar and the proverbial mysteries of Asia.

When I was done, I retrieved the samurai sword from my luggage and followed Sugimoto up to the *News Pop* studio, which was on the seventh floor of the building.

In Los Angeles I once saw a taping of a TV comedy. It was done in a sound stage big enough to hold three different sets and bleachers for a live audience. By comparison, the *News Pop* studio was minuscule. The studio was about the size of a large living room. In the high ceiling were a series of metal bars with a large assortment of lights clamped to them. Most of the floor space was taken up by cameras, and even the cameras were tiny. At the U.S. TV taping, the cameras were the size of briefcases, but the cameras used on *News Pop* were the size of a kid's lunch box. Three of these cameras were mounted on tubular tripods set on wheels so they could be moved around for different angles in front of the set.

About a half-dozen people were in the room. They seemed to be blocking out shots with a director, with cameramen taking instructions as they moved their cameras around the studio floor. A couple of technicians seemed to be repairing some cable that went from a desk with several monitors and disappeared into the floor. It was crowded.

The set for the program was jammed up against one wall. It was basically a counter with a *shōji* screen for a background. Several chairs were placed behind the counter. On the surface of the counter were glass panels that seemed to cover computer screens set into the desk. I surmised that notes or the script were flashed on these screens. *News Pop* had to be a "talking heads" show that relied on videotape for anything that required space or movement.

"I've got to tell them you're here and set up the promo. Then I'll introduce you to Nagahara-san and Yukiko-chan, our stars. In the meantime I'm going to introduce you to Junko Ohara, a researcher on the program. She helps with English-speaking guests."

Sugimoto called out to a woman who was conferring with the director. She was in her early thirties, dressed in a white long-sleeve blouse and gray skirt. Her hair was worn in a bob with bangs that reminded me of a 1920s flapper. She was about five feet tall and could probably stand to lose ten pounds, the same weighty crime I've already admitted to being guilty of.

"Junko-san, this is Mr. Tanaka, the detective from the United States," Sugimoto said.

"I'm not a detective," I interjected. "I'm a computer programmer who acted as an amateur sleuth."

"Amateur or professional, you're twelve minutes of next week's show and I'm pleased to meet you. My name is Junko Ohara." Her English was absolutely perfect. She extended her hand and I shook it.

"Why don't you two get acquainted while I go get Nagahara-san and Yukiko-chan. We'll get this promo piece shot and have you in your hotel in just a few minutes."

Sugimoto left us. Junko looked at me and said, "You look tired, but I wouldn't count on his promise that everything will be shot in just a few minutes. It's only a twenty-second promo, but it will take us an hour or more. Why don't you come to my desk and I'll get you some tea?"

"That sounds good. The offer of tea, I mean. Spending another hour or so here doesn't sound too good. My body thinks it's about three A.M."

Junko took me out of the studio and down a flight of stairs.

There she showed me into a large office space filled with tiny metal desks jammed together. Although it was past seven P.M. local time, there were still a lot of people in the office. Junko seated me at one of the small desks and went to get me a cup of Japanese green tea.

After thanking her for the tea, I said, "Your English is remarkably good. Did you live in the States at some time?"

"I wish," Junko said. "Actually I've never been out of Japan. I went to college at Sophia, which is a school in Tokyo where all lectures and classes are conducted in English. I also speak a good Spanish and a passable German. I guess I just have a good ear."

"Mr. Sugimoto said your last name was Ohara?"

"Just call him Buzz. He likes that. And yes, my last name is Ohara."

"In the U.S. that would be an Irish name."

"It's actually Korean. We pronounce it slightly differently than the Irish. We Koreans also have Lees, like your famous Civil War general, or maybe Spike Lee. You can't always tell from last names. Ohara could also be a Japanese name, but I'm still Korean."

"Now I'm confused," I admitted. "I thought you said you've never been out of Japan."

"That's right. I was born here, as were my mother and father."

"But wouldn't that make you Japanese?"

She gave a rueful laugh. "There are some things you have to learn about Japan. Just because you're born in Japan, that doesn't make you a Japanese citizen. You have to have a Japanese mother and a Japanese father to get automatic Japanese citizenship at birth. My family has been in Japan since the thirties, but we're still classified as foreigners and not citizens. I've actually never been to Korea and Korean isn't one of the languages I know, but I'm still a resident alien in Japan."

As an Asian in the United States, I knew what it was to be a minority. Junko's situation put a whole new light on minority status, however. Living two or three generations in a country and still being considered an alien resident was strange to me. The first generation of Japanese-Americans were prevented from becoming naturalized citizens until 1952, but at least their children, the *Nisei*, were born citizens.

She looked at me and said, "Look, instead of complaining about things, I should be teaching you your lines."

"Lines?"

"Yeah. During the promo we want you to say 'Please take a look,' in Japanese."

"But I don't speak Japanese."

"It's really simple. It's short and I'll teach it to you phonetically. Repeat after me, *goran, kudasai*."

"Goran, kudasai."

"Pretty good, but let's try it again. I'll give you a nice, high-class accent. Listen carefully. Goran, kudasai."

"Am I going to have to learn more Japanese for the show?"

"Oh, no. Everything will be translated for you. It's just that our research indicates that our shows with translations are usually less popular than shows where everything is conducted in Japanese. You look Japanese, so if you say something in Japanese in the promo, viewers will assume that the interview will be conducted in Japanese."

"Isn't that a little misleading?"

She sighed. "I see you're not familiar with television."

"No, I'm not."

"Do you object to saying something in Japanese during the promo?"

"No, I guess not," I said reluctantly.

"Good. Now listen carefully and try to imitate my intonation."

After we practiced the phrase to Junko's satisfaction, she asked me, "You said you're a computer programmer?"

"Yes, I am."

"Well, I have to do more research on your segment. Would you like to watch me access the English language databases we use?"

"Yes, that would be very interesting to me."

Junko took me over to a section of the office where there were three computers on little carts. In the U.S., each worker would have his or her own computer, but here computers seemed to be shared. The machines were already turned on, so she sat in front of one and started some kind of communications program.

Junko signed on to an English-language news database and entered a starting date and a few search words. She chose "murder," "sword," and "Japanese." After a few seconds, the message 14 STORIES FOUND appeared on the computer screen.

The stories were printed out on an old-fashioned, noisy, dot matrix printer. My illusions about a technologically advanced society in Japan were being shattered. Most personal computers sold for home use in the States seemed more advanced than the equipment being used by this big Japanese TV network.

Junko handed the stories to me. The longest were the L.A. *Times* pieces about the murder and my involvement in solving it. There was even a very small piece about the murder from *The New York Times* that I didn't know of. Three stories that had nothing to do with my murder case were printed out. They were printed because they met the search criteria Junko had entered.

REPUTED ORGANIZED CRIME FIGURE ASSASSINATED

NEW YORK (AP)—George "Georgie L." LaRusse, a reputed organized crime chief, was murdered last night in what police describe as one of the most spectacular gangland killings in years. The assailant entered LaRusse's forty-fourth floor high-security apartment by removing the glass from a window. Police speculate that the murderer may have been lowered to the apartment from the roof of the building by accomplices.

LaRusse was both stabbed and thrown out of the open window. Ironically, he landed on the hood of a police car driving by the building. Two officers in the car were unhurt. Police are currently uncertain of the motive for the assassination, but did say LaRusse had recently been involved in territorial disputes over crime activities in Harlem.

In a bizarre twist to the case, an ancient Japanese samurai sword was stolen from the apartment by the assassin. The sword was not used in the attack on LaRusse. Police found the knife used in the assassination still in the victim's body. According to Patricia King, manager of Derek Stacy Decorating, the company that decorated LaRusse's apartment, the sword is considered quite valuable. "It was purchased at auction for $11,000 and should be worth quite a bit more now. Mr. LaRusse insisted on the finest decor for his apartment, although he was not a collector or art connoisseur himself. The sword was a fine example of 17th-century Japanese swordmaking, by the swordsmith Kannemori." What connection, if any, the sword theft had to the assassination is still being investigated by the police.

LaRusse's career was free of convictions, despite his well-known association with organized crime and organized crime figures. LaRusse was connected to the protection racket, prostitution and the numbers racket. He was indicted once in 1979 in an assault case, but escaped conviction when both the victim and the only witness to the assault recanted their grand jury testimony at the trial. Prosecutors later hoped to secure an indictment against LaRusse for intimidating the witnesses, but had to abandon prosecution when the witnesses refused to cooperate.

THEFT OF RARE SWORD

ROTTERDAM (REUTERS)—A rare Japanese sword was stolen yesterday from the Dutch Shipping Museum. The sword was part of an exhibit on the Dutch presence in Nagasaki, Japan, at the beginning of the 17th century. Dutch police describe the sword as being made by the swordsmith Kannemori and quite valuable.

"I don't know why someone would steal such a distinctive sword," Wim Brock, the museum's director, said. "It will be murder to sell."

Authorities believe the theft may be an inside job because there was no evidence of forcible entry and the alarm system was operative. Although the investigation continues, police admit that they have no suspects at this time.

STUDENT IN BIZARRE 'SEX' DEATH

TOKYO (REUTERS)—A student suspected of stealing a rare 17th-century samurai sword from the Japan National Museum was found dead yesterday under bizarre circumstances. Yasuo Ishibashi, 19, was found strangled in a Japanese "love motel," and Tokyo police are uncertain how to characterize the death.

"It could be a suicide because of the trouble Mr. Ishibashi was in or it could be an accident involving strangulation for sexual pleasure. It could even be murder," commented Tokyo police inspector H. Hayase. "Right now, it's difficult to comment because of the strange circumstances."

Hayase said there was no suicide note and that Ishibashi was found hanging in front of a television showing pornographic movies. "There are actually some people who derive sexual pleasure from strangulation," commented Hayase, "and this may just be a bizarre accident involving this kind of practice."

Ishibashi's family said he was under considerable pressure because he was a suspect in the theft of a rare 17th-century samurai sword that was stolen from the Japan National Museum. The family said he was not suicidal and had no known proclivities for the kind of sexual perversion suggested by the police.

The sword, made by master swordsmith Kannemori, is considered a national treasure by the Japanese. The sword dates from the early 17th century, an era in Japanese history made popular by the novel and television show, *Shogun*. Ishibashi was working as a student volunteer at the museum and museum officials claim Ishibashi was the only one with access to this sword when it disappeared.

Ishibashi attended prestigious Waseda University in Tokyo. He took additional classes in Japanese history and martial arts at All Japan University, also in Tokyo.

"This is strange," I commented. "There seems to be an epidemic of deaths and sword thefts, and all are swords made by the same swordsmith. That's a peculiar connection."

Junko took the news stories from me and read them. She looked at me and shrugged. "Weird," she said.

Junko was right about the promotional piece taking more than an hour to organize and shoot. There was much shuffling around and a couple of false starts before we finally walked on the set and shot the promo. As befit the stars of the show, Nagahara-san and Yukiko-chan didn't show up on the set until we were actually ready to shoot.

The two hosts of the program were certainly an odd couple. Nagahara-san was a man in his late fifties with a somber face covered with age spots and a large mole on his upper lip. It occurred to me that in the U.S. a mole of that size would be removed for cosmetic purposes by most people, not just those in show business. His salt-and-pepper hair was closely cropped and his suit was crumpled. He looked like a local shopkeeper instead of a television personality, but maybe that was his appeal to Japanese audiences. Aside from "Hello," his English was almost nonexistent, and Junko translated his laconic greetings for me.

Yukiko-chan was a young woman who was probably in her midtwenties. *Chan* added to the end of a name is a diminutive usually reserved for children and women. Applied to women, it shows a linguistic mind-set that must drive Japanese feminists to despair. Yukiko-chan corrected me when I tried to call her Yukiko-*san,* however. She liked the chan honorific.

Her English was also poor, and when she saw me, she started speaking Japanese. I guess if you have a Japanese face, some people think you must speak Japanese. It's the reverse of what I experience in the U.S., where if you have an Asian face, some people don't think you can speak proper English. Like many Asian-Americans, I've actually been complimented on how well I speak English. When Yukiko-chan started in with Japanese, I gave her the kind of blank stare I usually reserve for people in the U.S. who think they have to speak pidgin English to me, only this time the stare was genuine. Junko gently inserted herself to translate.

Yukiko had a face that looked like a teenager's, and she was dressed in a short pink frilly dress that was styled like something the young Shirley Temple would have worn. Her hair was cut short and shaped to frame her tiny face, and when she talked she revealed crooked teeth. Japanese TV audiences seem to find crooked teeth cute. In different clothes Yukiko would look her age, but apparently she wanted to cultivate a little girl look. Her on-camera personality could only be described as perky, but away from the lens she seemed a bit petulant.

The promo was shot with Yukiko-chan and Nagahara-san sitting at the desk of the set like news anchors. They had me stand to one side of them, holding the blade of the sword with the tip resting on the desktop. Sugimoto suggested that it would be more dramatic if I removed the sword from the scabbard. When they played back the promo, which only lasted ten seconds, I must say I cut a dashing figure. Okay, maybe dashing is stretching things a bit, but I did think I looked just fine. Junko told me that my little statement in Japanese, which I got to say at the very end of the promo, sounded great and I must say I was pleased by that, too.

No matter how pleased I was, my body clock was telling me it was about five in the morning L.A. time, and when they finally got me bundled into the limo and over to the Imperial Hotel, I was exhausted.

The Imperial Hotel is across from Hibiya Park and very near the Imperial Palace. It was originally designed by Frank Lloyd Wright and was famous for surviving the great 1926 Tokyo earthquake. Wright's design may have withstood earthquakes, but it couldn't survive urban renewal, Japanese style. The original building was torn down in the sixties and a new hotel was built on the same site. Later a tower was added to the main hotel, but Sugimoto said the show got me a room in the older section because the rooms were much bigger. I don't know if that's true, but by that time, I was just interested in a room with a bed.

The room was nice, but not spectacular. It had a small couch and the usual overpriced minibar. If you ignored the package of dried squid snacks I found in the minibar, it was a room that wouldn't be distinctive in L.A. or New York or Cleveland.

Before I went to bed, I filled out a card for a breakfast to be delivered to my room at 9 A.M. the following morning. I noted with a little shock that with the current exchange rate, a modest egg breakfast cost around $35. I also noted with amusement that the little check boxes for breakfast delivery indicated times that were ten minutes apart. I smiled at this phony precision and changed my time selection to 9:10 A.M. When I finally crawled into bed, I immediately dropped off into a deep and dreamless sleep.

A knocking at my door woke me. I pried open my eyes and looked at the clock on the bedstand. Precisely 9:10 A.M. A little groggy and bemused, I opened the door to a waiter standing next to a cart holding my breakfast.

As I ate, I turned on the television. The hotel had an English language channel, but it was playing an incredibly boring interview with a visiting Christian missionary. I would think missionary work could be interesting and exciting, but the interview featured a great deal of bureaucratic mumbling about the details of the missionary's trip and almost nothing in the way of interesting stories or observations.

I turned the channel to the network that ran News Pop, and although everything was in Japanese and I didn't understand a word, I still found it more interesting. The Japanese shows seemed to start at odd times, like 9:35, instead of regular hourly or half-hourly intervals. They had more commercials, but individual advertisers seemed to run shorter commercials. An advertiser might run the same commercial two or even three times in a row, however. With some of the commercials, it was hard to figure out what they were trying to sell because the pictures seemed to have nothing to do with the product. They might show a picture of rain in a pine forest and at the last minute pitch you to buy shoes. Maybe if I understood Japanese the relationships would be clear, but trying to figure out what I was seeing was still amusing. One thing that was very exciting was seeing the promo I shot the previous night. In the forty-five minutes or so I watched TV, I saw it run twice.

It was around 10 A.M., which meant it was 5 P.M. in Los Angeles. Mariko had told me to call her to let her know I had arrived safely. I knew she was waiting for my call so I picked up a card by the phone and read how to make a long distance call to the Kawashiri Boutique, where she worked when she wasn't looking for acting jobs.

Mariko is in her midthirties, so she's a bit younger than I. She worked for most of her life at a bank and decided a few years ago that she wanted to be an actress. She also realized she had a drinking problem and got active in AA. She reshaped her life by her own choice and I admired her for it. With the loss of my job, my life was changed through the actions of others and I was still trying to figure out how I was going to cope.

I guess changing our careers and lifestyles two or three times during the course of our lives is no longer unusual in the United States. Internal changes and external changes demand this from increasing numbers of us. Mariko and I have both had failed marriages, so we've both already had major changes in the course of our lives. For me, finding Mariko was another major change and the longer I know her, the more I realize how profound that change is.

I started punching numbers on the phone, using the U.S. country code, the area code, and the boutique's phone number. She picked it up after only a couple of rings.

"Hello, Kawashiri Boutique," she said. Pretty mundane, but her voice sounded like the sweetest poetry to me.

"It's me. I got here uneventfully and I've already seen myself on Japanese TV pitching the show."

"I'm glad you called. I miss you already."

"You should have gone into hock and joined me."

"Don't tempt me. It's just too much money."

"That's true. My breakfast this morning cost around thirty-five dollars for eggs and toast. That's about fifteen dollars per egg and five dollars for the toast."

"So the beautiful pearl necklace I was expecting is out?"

"Don't worry. I haven't done any shopping, but I'm sure I can find a lovely souvenir T-shirt for you."

"You don't have to bring anything back for me except yourself," she said. "Just come back safe."

"That's no worry. I'm here in Tokyo, the safest big city in the world."

"Tell that to the thousands gassed by that Japanese cult. Speaking of safety, I had some excitement here last night."

"What happened?"

"Mrs. Hernandez called the police because she thought someone was breaking into your apartment."

Mrs. Hernandez is my neighbor in the duplex I rent. She has a good heart, but she's a snoop. When I'm doing the snooping, it's okay. When I'm being snooped on, it's annoying. I've left my apartment at 6 in the morning and returned at 2 A.M. the following morning and she's commented on it, including the exact times I left and returned. She's retired and has nothing better to do than to watch the comings and goings of her neighbors. The positive part about her is that she is superior to any home alarm system.

"What happened?"

"She was convinced that someone was prowling around your apartment late last night, so first she called the police and then she called me."

"Why did she call you?"

"She knows I have a key to your apartment. She wanted me to come and let the police into your apartment."

"I'm surprised she hasn't had a key made for herself, just so she can snoop at leisure. Did you go down?"

"Of course. We went in and looked around, but I saw nothing out of place and the police saw no signs of a forced entry. At least your apartment didn't look like Cathy's."

Cathy was a friend of Mariko's who was called at work by the police and asked to return home because her apartment had been burglarized. That morning Cathy was rushed and late for work, so she actually ran out of her apartment without properly slamming the door behind her. A neighbor noticed her door was ajar and peeked through the open door to see if everything was okay. What the neighbor saw caused him to call the police.

When Cathy got home, there were two police cars and four police officers waiting. A female police officer pulled Cathy aside and said to her, "We want you to enter your apartment to see what's missing. Please don't touch anything because we want to dust for fingerprints." The officer hesitated a moment, then said, "You might want to prepare yourself for a few seconds before you go in. I've been inside and they pretty well trashed your apartment looking for valuables. Things are thrown everywhere and it's a complete a mess, so watch where you step."

Cathy braced herself and stepped into an apartment with clothes and other belongings tossed on the floor and spread around the apartment. Then she had to brace herself a second time to tell the police officers that nothing was missing and that was how she normally kept her apartment.

I started laughing and said, "That story about Cathy was the reason I cleaned things up before I left for Japan. I thought if any-body did go into the apartment, I didn't want to be accused of felony sloppiness. So there was no burglar after all?"

"I guess not. I think Mrs. Hernandez must be losing it. She rousted me out of a sound sleep for no good reason."

"That's very strange. She's usually very accurate. She acts as a one-woman neighborhood watch and not too much goes on that she doesn't notice. If she said there was a prowler, I'd tend to believe her."

"She said the prowler got into your apartment, but when we looked, there was absolutely no sign that anyone had been in there. If someone did get into your apartment, they decided there was nothing worth stealing."

"It's still strange," I said.

"So, what's on the schedule today?" Mariko asked, changing the subject.

"Cheap sightseeing, if I can swing it, and a stop by the studio this afternoon."

"Well, have fun, and come home safely to me. I love you."

"I love you, too."

A lthough *News Pop* was picking up my tab for travel, hotel rooms, and meals, all sightseeing was to be done on my own nickel. I was still living off the settlement given me when the Calcommon Corporation downsized my job out of existence, so although I could expect a check for a few more months, I didn't have money to burn.

There's a large shopping arcade under the Imperial Hotel, and after changing some traveler's checks for yen in the lobby, I went down to the arcade as my first stop. I passed the fancy art galleries, designer clothing stores, and nice restaurants and made my way to a bookstore. At the bookstore, I bought a good street map of Tokyo and had the clerk circle the location of the Imperial Hotel.

I figured if I got really lost, I could point to the circle on the map and a taxi driver could get me back to the hotel. Of course, that might not always work. I heard a story of a tourist in Tokyo who picked up a matchbook in his hotel's lobby, figuring that if he ever became lost he could point to the hotel's name on the matchbook and have the taxi driver take him back to the hotel.

The inevitable happened and the tourist became hopelessly lost. He jumped into a taxi and handed the matchbook to the driver. The driver asked a question in Japanese and the tourist replied in English. It took about two seconds to realize that neither person could speak the other's language. The tourist kept pointing to the matchbook and gesturing until the taxi driver had a light bulb go on. "Ah!" the driver exclaimed and he started driving. The tourist settled back in the cab and relaxed while the driver drove for about thirty minutes.

Suddenly the taxi came to a stop in an industrial neighborhood that was totally unfamiliar to the tourist. He was trying to figure out where he was while the driver proudly pointed to a building in front of the cab. The tourist looked out of the cab and saw a factory building with a big sign on it that said Tokyo Match Company.

My map had a diagram of the large Tokyo subway and rail system on it. One elevated train, the Yamanote line, runs in a huge circle around Tokyo. This circular line is sometimes used in Japan to describe a speaker. If a speaker is a Yamanote, it means he goes around and around and never comes to the point. I thought riding a loop on the Yamanote line would be a cheap way to get a quick tour of the city. I checked my map and decided to walk to a nearby train station, hop on the Yamanote line, and ride it until I had made a complete circle before getting off at the station next to where I got on.

Walking to the train station from the hotel was an interesting experience. I thought that some racial memory might make the streets of Japan familiar, but although I felt oddly comfortable on the streets, Tokyo was as alien to me as Lagos, Nigeria, or Bombay, India would be.

The twisty streets of Tokyo, originally laid out in a way to confound invading armies, also serve to confound invading tourists. The fact that some streets don't have names also adds to the fun, along with the Japanese custom of assigning numbers based on the sequence that the buildings in a neighborhood were built. Over time, this custom makes it impossible to guarantee that building four is flanked by buildings three and five. For a country normally viewed by the rest of the world as being orderly and systematic, something as simple as trying to find an address illustrates that the Japanese are as illogical and silly as the rest of us.

As I walked along, the people around me seemed to be in a great rush. In Los Angeles, we sort of meander when we walk.

In Tokyo, people were very intent on reaching their destination and not intent on enjoying the journey. As I walked along, I wondered if I was doing the *gin-bura*, or Ginza stroll. In the old days, the samurai would positively swagger, especially on a big public street in the Ginza district, where all the big money lenders, banks, and smartest shops could be found. Now it looked more to me like the Japanese were practicing the Ginza sprint, because I was the only one strolling.

As people scurried past me, they treated me very much like a tree or one of the metal guardrails that seemed designed to keep people from parking on the sidewalk. The bustle was very reminiscent of New York City, but with one big difference. In Tokyo, not one person bumped into me, jostled me, or even gave me a hard look. The schools of people seemed to flow around me like fish around coral.

I made it to the train station, bought a ticket from a machine, and climbed up to the platform. The train was old, but kept up, and for once I had a good time running around in circles. I ended up in the Ginza, near where I started from, and spent the rest of the day exploring the area and wandering through the big department stores.

For lunch I stopped at the restaurant in the Wako department store that looks over the intersection of Chuo Dori and Harumi Dori, the heart of the Ginza. I ate tiny cucumber, butter, and ham sandwiches that had the crusts carefully sliced off and watched the endless ebb and flow of humanity outside the window.

In the crowd, I saw a tall blond tourist making his way across the intersection. His pale skin, straw hair, and lanky body looked totally out of place in the milling crowd of short, dark-haired pedestrians. He was a pale cork bobbing in a sea of black and brown. I realized that the reason I felt comfortable on the streets was because I blended into the crowd perfectly. That's not always an advantage in Japan. I know another AJA (American of Japanese Ancestry) who frequently comes to Japan on business. He once told me that he liked to walk with tall, blond business associates because the Tokyo drivers will always stop and let a *gaijin* (foreigner) cross the street. Because he looked Japanese, my friend was cut no slack by Tokyo drivers, and he was expected to be nimble and watch out for himself when crossing the road.

Junko would be able to blend into this street scene as easily as I would, but in Japan she was an alien. I was used to standing out based on my Asian looks, and I associated racial prejudice with looking different. When I was in the army during the Vietnam War, I was once sitting on the ground with a large number of recruits early in my stint in basic training. A grizzled sergeant came up to us and barked, "Tanaka! Stand up!" I didn't know what I had done wrong, but I scrambled to my feet as ordered. "Okay, you recruits, look at Tanaka. Take a good look, because this is what a gook looks like, and gooks are the enemy!" My faced burned, but I was nineteen and in the midst of the most frightening and unsettling experience of my life and didn't know what to do. All I could do was stand there humiliated as the other recruits laughed. What was especially disturbing was this sergeant was African-American, and he must have known what it was like to be singled out because of your race. Unfortunately, whatever life experiences he had along these lines didn't teach him empathy, only mimicry.

Junko looked just like the people walking around on the street below me. Yet despite looking, acting, and sounding like everyone else, she was a minority because her ancestors were born in Korea. It's a strange world, and one we make unnecessarily stranger by dividing people up into different types of minorities.

In the afternoon, I took a cab back to the studio and met with a pleasant surprise from Junko. As soon as she saw me, she asked, "Where did you say you bought that sword?"

"At a garage sale."

"And how much did you pay for it?"

"A hundred dollars."

"When we leave the studio I want you to go with me to buy a lottery ticket," Junko said.

"Why?"

"Because you must be incredibly lucky. That sword could be very valuable."

Stunned, I asked, "How do you know?"

"Those news stories we found made me curious about who

the swordsmith Kannemori was and why so many of his swords were stolen, so I did some research against some Japanese language databases. Those databases are more comprehensive than the English language databases we subscribe to. In the university database, I found an article about Kannemori swords that was printed in a scholarly journal in 1987. It described some unusual swords made by Kannemori in the early 1600s. It seems the swords were especially made for the Toyotomi clan. These blades have a design incised into the blades that actually weakens the sword and ruins it as a fighting weapon. Your sword has the same kind of designs as those described in the article. The article talked about blades at the Japan National Museum and in the hands of a private collector here in Japan. Those two had different designs on their blades and yours seems to be different still. If yours is a Kannemori blade it could be worth a lot."

"How could we find out for sure?"

"I've already called the author of the article, Professor Hirota. He teaches Japanese history at All Japan University. He's out of town right now, but his assistant said Professor Hirota would call me as soon as he's back. He said the professor would probably be very interested. I'm going to ask Professor Hirota if he'll look at your sword and see if it's a Kannemori."

I don't view myself as a greedy man, but I was unemployed and the prospect of a windfall from a garage sale purchase made my spirits soar.

Junko was working on a videotape piece that gave the details of the murder I had solved, and she asked me to help make sure the chronology and facts were right. She was weaving news footage and stock pictures of Los Angeles together to illustrate the piece, which she said would take up three minutes of my twelve-minute segment. I secretly wished she would make a longer tape introduction, because the remaining nine minutes of live interview seemed like an eternity to fill.

My enthusiasm for being on camera live was waning as I thought of all the embarrassing and disastrous possibilities. Mostly, I thought I'd freeze up and sit there grinning like an idiot while the hosts asked me questions in Japanese. Finally I confessed my apprehensions to Junko.

She smiled and said, "Everyone gets nervous, but not too many people admit it, especially men. You'll do fine. If you'd like, I'll give you some hints."

"*Dōzo,*" I said, using the Japanese word for please.

"I thought you didn't speak Japanese," she answered.

"Dōzo represents a significant chunk of my Japanese vocabulary. I know some words, but I don't know grammar. Plus, everyone speaks so fast, I can't even pick out the few words I know."

Junko laughed. "When you're beginning to learn a language, it seems like everyone is speaking really fast. It's just that you haven't adjusted to the rhythm of the language yet. After a while, it seems like people slow down and you can hear individual words, but it's really because you've picked up an ear for a particular language."

"You should know. You speak several languages."

"Well, the more you learn, the easier it seems. Everyone gets English training in the Japanese school system, although English teachers are usually terrible. We learn to read and write it very well, but spoken language skills are incredibly poor. Many of our English teachers just don't know how to speak it properly."

"Japanese is a hard language. I've thought of trying to learn it, but it seems too difficult."

"Japanese is hard, but its main problem is that it has little utility outside of Japan. English, Spanish, or French are used in many countries, so they're much more useful than Japanese. Actually, English is incredibly hard to learn well because you have a huge vocabulary and similar words are pronounced differently. Also, you have sounds in English that we seldom use in Japanese. Spanish is popular here because its sounds are closer to Japanese and a lot easier for us to pronounce."

"Then you'd get along in L.A. Spanish is the second language."

"Since we're working on a piece about the murder of a Japanese in L.A., I'm not sure I'm anxious to visit it. L.A. has a terrible reputation for safety here in Japan."

"Well, with subway gassings and other violence Tokyo is losing its reputation for safety, too."

Junko sighed. "Yes, I guess you're right. Maybe there aren't any places for safety left in this world."

"There are, but they're not to be found in big cities. Can I ask you something?"

"What is it?"

"When you were talking about Japanese learning English you said 'we,' but you made a point of telling me you were Korean when we met. Do you consider yourself Japanese?"

"That's hard to know. Sometimes it seems like Japanese society makes a point of emphasizing I'm Korean. Koreans are often discriminated against, and it's hard to find a good job because Koreans are often relegated to hard and dirty work. I'm an exception, but I've had to work twice as hard as any Japanese to make the same progress. Koreans have the reputation of being connected with Japanese organized crime and caught up in gambling, prostitution, and extortion, and some employers just won't hire us."

"Are Koreans involved in crime?"

Junko turned red. "Koreans are involved in greater numbers than our share of the population. Part of that is because many legitimate avenues for advancement are closed to us. But a lot of Japanese are involved in crime and Koreans seem to be treated more harshly when they're caught."

"That's exactly the view of some minorities in the States. Why don't you try to take political action or something to change things? Shake things up a bit?"

"Because in Japan, harmony is valued above all. We have radical groups on the right and on the left, but generally speaking most people are very conservative and don't want to shake things up, as you put it. There's also a practical reason. Japanese politics requires huge amounts of money."

"It does in the U.S., too. But instead of seeking harmony we're becoming increasingly factionalized. That doesn't make it pleasant for Asians or other minority groups who can't get a block vote together."

"But in the U.S., your government has still made periodic efforts to correct some inequities. In Japan, the government won't even acknowledge problems. Japan occupied Korea as a colonial power for about thirty-five years after World War I. That's why my grandfather was brought here as a virtual slave laborer. In Korea, the Korean language was forbidden and the population was oppressed. Korean women were forced to become comfort women, which is a Japanese euphemism for prostitutes. The Japanese government has just acknowledged that practice, but they've never compensated the women. They said a private fund, not the government, should do that. They spent $600 million to promote the fund and collected only about half that much in donations. It was a complete farce. The history I was taught in school just didn't chronicle the bad things the Japanese did."

"When I grew up, they didn't teach about the U.S. camps for Japanese-Americans during World War II, either," I said. "Now the U.S. government has made some effort to compensate the camp inmates. But Junko, if things are so difficult for you in Japan, why do you stay?"

"Because culturally I'm Japanese. Although I was born a Korean, my native language, schooling, and much of my outlook is Japanese. It's confusing because I also want to remain Korean. I just feel like I'm not accepted for what I am."

"I sometimes have the same feelings back in the States."

J unko asked me to return the next afternoon to help her. Before I left, Sugimoto stopped by and asked me if I'd like to
have dinner the next day. I told him I would, but that I wanted
to go to a typical family restaurant, not one of the fancy tourist
traps. He looked a little disappointed, and it occurred to me that
maybe he liked the tourist traps because he could eat at the neighborhood joints anytime. Still, on my own I wasn't likely to find
a good neighborhood restaurant, and I suppressed my urge to
change my restaurant request.

I left the studio around six and decided to walk back to the
hotel. I wanted to absorb more of the atmosphere of the city. I
strolled out of the studio and started walking. People were getting out of work and rushing about. I enjoyed the pulse and energy around me.

I had walked about two blocks when an elderly woman came
rushing up to me. She was dressed in *kimono,* and I realized she
was the first person I had seen in traditional Japanese dress. Her
kimono was brown with a dark brown *obi,* or sash. She was carrying a bundle in a purple *furoshiki.* She was chubby, with red
cheeks and glossy black hair fixed in a bun. She looked as if she'd
normally be quite jolly, but now she looked frazzled and a little
lost.

She said something to me in rapid-fire Japanese, bobbing
up and down as she apologized for something. I realized the

apology was probably for bothering me, but I had no idea what she wanted.

I said, "Watashi wa Nihongo ga wakarimasen." That's a stock phrase I memorized from a guidebook, and it means I don't speak Japanese. For some reason, my words didn't register with her. She just heard me speaking Japanese and starting talking even more rapidly.

I put my hands up and said, "Do you speak English?"

The woman looked surprised and said something else to me in Japanese.

"I'm afraid I don't understand you. Watashi wa Nihongo ga wakarimasen. I'm an American."

"American!" the woman exclaimed. Then she started laughing.

The woman thought for a minute, then she made a choo-choo pantomime with her arms, puffing like a little steam engine. I realized she wanted to find the nearest train station and I smiled. I pulled out my tourist map of Tokyo and opened it up. It took a few seconds to orient myself and find the exact street corner we were standing on. I found the nearest train station and asked, "Yurakucho?" Yurakucho was the name of the train that stopped at the nearest station.

"Yurakucho!" she repeated, all excited. I had hit paydirt.

I rapidly turned around to point out the direction she should go to reach the station. As I turned, I noticed two men standing by a shop window watching me. One was short and stocky with muscular shoulders bunched up under a cheap tan suit. His hair was closely cropped. The other man was tall and gaunt, wearing a rumpled gray suit and a knit shirt that seemed yellow with age. What caught my eye was that as soon as I turned, they both started looking into the shop window intently. It was a woman's dress shop and their show of interest seemed both incongruous and false. I figured they were watching the little show the woman and I were putting on and were embarrassed at being caught. The old woman's imitation of a train was pretty amusing and I didn't blame them for their interest. I pointed out the direction and held up three fingers to indicate three blocks. Then I pointed to the map and counted off *"Ichi, ni, san"* or "one, two, three" in Japanese, as I indicated the blocks to the train station.

The woman giggled and nodded her comprehension at my instructions. Then she bowed and thanked me profusely. I caught several *arigato*s, which is thank you in Japanese. She bustled off in the direction I had pointed to and I continued my walk to the hotel.

I strolled along for a couple of more blocks until I saw a *Pachinko* parlor. In Pachinko, little metal balls are shot into the air and come cascading down into various wheels, mechanical flowers, and cups. When a ball goes into one of the cups a bell rings, lights flash, and additional balls pour out of the machine. It's sort of a cross between pinball and a slot machine. You can use the balls you've won to play some more or you can trade them in for gifts of various sorts. I've read you can even trade in your winnings for money, although this is supposed to be illegal because this would make Pachinko a gambling game instead of a game of amusement.

On a whim, I ducked into the Pachinko parlor to see this phenomenon close up. Rows of machines were tightly crowded in aisles, with pink plastic stools in front of them. Players were sitting on the stools in front of their machines, intently watching the trajectory of the balls being shot up into the machine. Pachinko used to be manually operated, but these machines were all automated. By turning a big wheel, the force used to shoot the balls to the top of the machine could be varied, and this is where the skill, such as it was, came in. The noise of all the machines was terrific, but the players seemed totally oblivious as they watched the machines in front of them. One guy had an enormous number of metal balls coming out of his machine. I watched him for several minutes because he had the knack for positioning the balls in just the right place so that when they cascaded down the machine, they had the highest likelihood of hitting something that would pay off.

A player behind me started cursing and I turned around in time to see the last of his metal balls disappear into the bottom of the machine without hitting anything that would return more balls. I guess there is some skill to playing this. I looked up from the defeated player and saw the backs of two men at the end of the aisle of machines. I was sure they were the same two men who were studying the dress shop window when I had my encounter with the old lady. My level of concern shot up like the cascade of metal balls in the Pachinko machine.

I turned and made my way down the aisle and out of the shop. I strolled along, keeping to well-populated streets with plenty of people. I turned a corner and took a quick peek down the street I had just turned off from. The two men were coming down the street after me.

Tokyo is known as one of the safest big cities in the world, with very little street crime. Still, little street crime is very different than no street crime and I was being followed by two unsavory-looking characters. Maybe it was coincidence and maybe it wasn't. I didn't like the possibilities if it wasn't.

In Tokyo neighborhoods they have mini–police stations where the officers assigned to a neighborhood stay. Unfortunately, these stations weren't marked on my map and I had no idea how I'd go about finding one. I thought about going into an open business, but I wasn't sure I could communicate with the shopkeeper. Besides, the two guys had already followed me into the Pachinko parlor and I wasn't sure ducking into a shop would shake them. So, I just kept walking, doing my best to not look over my shoulder and tip them off that I had spotted them.

Acting normal in abnormal circumstances is hard. I wanted to break into a run, but I wasn't sure that was the best tactic. Ahead I saw the train station I had directed the old woman to. It was the tail end of rush hour and there were still large numbers of people streaming into the station. I entered the train station, pausing briefly to buy a ticket from one of the numerous machines lining the walls of the station entrance. Tokyo has a subway system, but the trains are on elevated tracks, like the El in Chicago. I joined the crowd going up the stairs to the platform where you get on the train.

I stood in the crowd waiting for the next train and chanced a quick look around. The two men were standing a few feet to my left. In a minute, a train came by the platform and stopped. A few people got off the train and as soon as they were clear the crowd moved forward as a single mass and squeezed onto the train. Once I got in the door, I stepped to one side, jamming up against a middle-aged businessman who glared at me. The crowd behind me continued to pack the train until I literally was immobile from the crush of bodies around me. They have that old saying about being packed like sardines, but sardines are dead when they're put in a can. The people in the train car were alive. So far.

A bell rang and the doors closed. The train lurched off. I didn't need to hang onto a strap or pole to stay upright. The truth is I was wedged in so tight I couldn't have fallen to the floor if I had wanted to. I had hoped that my two shadows might not get on the train, but I was able to see them near the other door of the car.

We went to the next station and once again a few people got off but even more people got on. I braced myself and resisted all efforts from the boarding crowd to push me away from the door. I guess this is against Tokyo train packing etiquette because I had several people scowl at me as they pushed past me to get into the car. As we took off, I stole a glance at the two men and realized that the rush had moved them further into the car.

At the next station, I waited until the debarking and boarding passengers did their thing. Once again, it was hard to stand my ground and stay near the entrance to the car, but I managed to. From riding the Yamanote line, I knew the sequence when a train departed from the station. First they rang a bell and a voice came across the public address system. Then the doors rapidly closed as the train took off. The bell went off and I pushed my way past a young woman and a teenager who were standing between me and the door. The closing door nipped at my heels as I burst out of the car and onto the platform. A blue-uniformed platform attendant came toward me saying something in Japanese, no doubt scolding me for waiting until the last second to get off the car. I didn't pay any attention. Instead I was staring through the windows of the departing car, looking at the two men who were stuck in the crowd like flies in amber. They abandoned all pretense of not being interested in me and stared at me with blank expressions. I wondered if I was mistaken about the men following me, but they pivoted their heads to watch me as the car went past. I couldn't resist waving good-bye to them, a big grin on my face.

I left the platform and immediately bought another ticket for a train going back to the station where I originally got on. This train was as packed as the other, but somehow I could breathe a lot better. When I got off, I flagged down a cab to take me to the hotel. Through a mechanical contraption, the driver was able to open the back door of the cab for me without getting out. "*Teikoku* Hotel," I said, mixing the Japanese word for Imperial with the English word *hotel*. The driver understood my linguistic amalgam and took off. I sat back into the plastic-covered seat of the cab and reflected that I liked walking in Tokyo, but I didn't like being stalked.

I woke up around 3 A.M. and couldn't get back to sleep. It was midmorning California time and I was wide awake. I called Mariko at the Kawashiri Boutique, and got Mrs. Kawashiri, the owner.

"Ken-san! I'm so glad to hear your voice. Are you calling from Tokyo?"

"Yes, I am. It's the middle of the night here, but I can't sleep. I slept fine the first night, but I guess I was just exhausted by the trip. I'm sorry to bother Mariko at work."

"Don't be silly. You can always call Mariko here, you know that. I'll go get her. She'll be thrilled."

When Mariko got on the line she did seem thrilled. I realized how much I missed her.

"Ken," she said, "it must be the middle of the night there. Has something happened?"

"No, it's just hard to sleep. It will take a few days to get adjusted to the time shift. I'll be adjusted just when it's time to come home. Oh, something almost did happen. I almost got mugged in what's supposed to be one of the safest cities in the world."

"What happened?"

"Nothing. Two guys just followed me. I managed to lose them on a train. It wasn't a big deal."

"I wish you wouldn't tell me about things like this. Now I'll be worried sick until you get home."

"Now I'm sorry I told you."

"Are you seeing anything neat?"

"Yesterday I rode around Tokyo on a train, then I explored the Ginza. I saw the old Kabuki theater and wandered through department stores."

"Did you see a Kabuki play?"

"No, I just looked at the theater. Maybe later this week I'll have the time. Everything is so expensive here. It's unbelievable. Even with the TV show picking up my room and meals, I have to budget pretty carefully. What do you have planned?"

"Mary Maloney and I are going to dinner."

Mary was helpful when I was trying to unravel the real murder I got involved in. She, Mariko, and I had become closer through that experience, but she wasn't someone I expected Mariko to pal around with.

"That's a surprise."

"She called me and suggested it. She knew you were in Japan and said I must be lonely. I am. I've been meaning to get together with her for some time now and I was happy she called."

Mary lived in a small house in South Pasadena that was stuffed with artwork. She said it wasn't too expensive when her father bought most of it many years ago. That might have been true years ago, but it wasn't true now. I estimated that there was literally millions of dollars worth of art in Mary's unassuming house.

"I like Mary, too, although I really don't know much about her. I hope you two have fun."

"What's on your agenda?"

"I plan to go to Ueno Park and the museums there. I have to check into the studio every afternoon to help on the segment they're doing on me. After that I'll have dinner with Buzz Sugimoto."

"What's he like?"

"Well, he's a bit odd. He's in his thirties and he dresses like James Dean. You know, jeans, cowboy boots, and white T-shirt. He even wears his hair in a 1950s jellyroll. His English is good, so I'm looking forward to talking to him."

"Well, have fun."

"Oh!"

"What is it?"

"I almost forgot the most exciting news of all."

"More exciting than potential muggings?"

"Yes, because this news means money."

"Some producer has seen your TV piece and wants you to star in a Japanese soap opera."

"Get serious. The researcher on the *News Pop* show says the sword I bought may be rare and could be worth a lot of money."

"Like millions?"

"Probably thousands, but certainly a lot more than I paid for it."

"That is exciting!"

We said the usual lovey-dovey things you say and I hung up. I watched some TV to kill time. They run English language movies late at night in the hotel, probably because difficulty adjusting to the time shift is a common occurrence. There was a button on the TV where you could hear the original English soundtrack or a dubbed Japanese version. We have the same thing in Los Angeles, where you can hear many programs in English or Spanish.

They were playing the original *Alien* with Sigourney Weaver, one of my favorite science fiction films. I also like *Them*, starring Jim Arness and giant ants, and a whole host of old Japanese movies like *Rodan* (it inspired me to learn how to spell *pterodactyl* long before dinosaurs became popular), *Gammera* (who could not like a giant, spinning, jet-propelled turtle?), and *Godzilla* (the original English-language version, not the 1985 remake). In other words, I'm a film buff. I watched Sigourney dodge the creepy alien until I got sleepy again, and nodded off before she was finally able to blast the creature into outer space.

The next morning, the rigors of foreign travel didn't look too stressful in the face of the really foreign travel of science fiction films. I ate another expensive breakfast and spent the day in Ueno Park looking at museums. In the late afternoon, I went to the studio and met with Junko. She said she was still waiting to hear back from the professor, but that she wanted to incorporate some information about the sword during the interview.

Buzz Sugimoto met me at Junko's desk. He was dressed just as I saw him at the airport, looking like an Asian, and aging, James Dean. As promised, he said he would take me to a real family-style Tokyo restaurant and we took the Yamanote line to Meguro station. From there, it was just a minute's walk to the restaurant.

The restaurant was large, cheerful, and crowded. Diners sat at a long polished wooden counter while the cooks worked on the other side. The specialty of the house was *tonkatsu,* a breaded pork cutlet, deep-fried and served with a special sauce on a bed of finely shredded cabbage. The restaurant's name, Tonki, fit with the name of the dish.

"I used to come here in my student days," Buzz said. "This is a typical neighborhood restaurant here in Tokyo, quite different than the ones we normally go to when we're on expense account." We had to wait for a place, sitting along the wall with about thirty other people. There seemed to be a constant ebb and flow of people entering and leaving the restaurant.

"How do we know when it's our turn?" I asked.

"The woman by the cash register saw us enter. When it's our turn she'll call us up."

I was a little skeptical of the woman's ability to keep all the new arrivals in order without notes or even a glance towards the door as new customers came in, but sure enough, we were called up in the proper sequence.

The pork cutlets were cooked in front of us in large vats of hot oil. The cooks were all veterans with hands scarred pink and brown from splattering oil. They worked over the vats using extremely long metal chopsticks, seemingly oblivious to the heat and jumping oil from the vats. I thought this might be a boring job, but many Japanese craftsmen seem to have a very Zen-like approach to this kind of career, carefully perfecting their craft though diligent repetition. It's something we seem to have forgotten in the U.S., where we're always seeking novelty in the things we do. The thought of spending a lifetime to perfect something as simple as frying a pork cutlet is a notion we can't fathom.

There's a story about old-time Tokyo oil sellers that illustrates this attitude. In the 1920s these peddlers used to walk around neighborhoods with a big jug of oil slung on their backs, crying out their wares. A local resident would come out with a pot to buy oil, and the seller would tip the big jug and pour out the purchased oil into the pot. One local oil seller was famous because he would take a Japanese coin that has a small 1/8-inch hole in the center and pour the oil through the hole without getting any on the coin. A visiting tourist once saw this demonstration and exclaimed, "What skill!" The oil seller looked at the tourist and said, "That is not skill. It is practice."

The food was good and filling and I decided that fast-food tonkatsu could be a big money maker in the states. During the dinner, I mentioned the two muggers and I asked Sugimoto if he thought I should report the incident to the police.

"You want to stay away from Japanese cops. They're terrible."

"What do you mean?" I was surprised.

"There's a story about an emperor in China who had three suspects for a crime," Sugimoto said. "The emperor didn't know who the real criminal was, but he knew one of the three had to be guilty. Instead of finding out who the guilty one was he simply had all three killed. In the West, you worry about protecting the rights of the innocent. Here in Japan, the cops are more interested in closing a case. They're like that Chinese emperor. They'd rather kill innocent men and close the case."

I looked incredulous, so Sugimoto continued. "Do you remember the Matsumoto poisoning case?"

"Is that the one with the doomsday cult?"

"That's right, the Aum Supreme Truth, the same cult that released the poison gas in the Tokyo subways. Matsumoto is a small town. One night a cloud of poison Sarin nerve gas rolled over a neighborhood in Matsumoto and seven people died. Hundreds of others were sickened. In that neighborhood lived a judge who had given a judgment against Aum. We know now that Aum wanted to test its nerve gas on people, and they figured they could literally kill two objectives if they released the gas in the judge's neighborhood.

"After the attack in Matsumoto, the police were puzzled. They didn't make the link between Aum and the judge, even though at least one newspaper reported it. Instead of tracking down Aum and perhaps preventing the Tokyo disaster, the police decided to close the case by saying a man named Kono caused the cloud of poison gas by mixing garden chemicals to make a weed killer. Scientists from all over Japan pointed out it was absurd to think that an amateur gardener could accidentally make a sophisticated nerve gas in a potting shed, but the police stuck to their theory and even extracted a confession out of Kono-san. I don't know how they got that confession, but Kono-san recanted it later. Anyway, after the Tokyo gassing, they quietly dropped the case against Kono-san, but they were quite willing to prosecute an innocent man to close the Matsumoto case. The Japanese legal system has something like a ninety-nine percent conviction rate on criminal cases, mostly based on confessions by the people charged."

"So the bottom line is, you don't think I should report my incident to the police?"

"Nothing good can come of it and maybe something bad might happen. The police aren't going to do anything. Two guys seemed to chase you, but you don't know why. It was an unpleasant chance encounter, and I'm sorry it scared you."

"Excuse me for saying this, but the Japanese legal system doesn't sound too attractive."

Sugimoto hesitated, but since I had plunged in, he decided he could speak frankly, too. "Actually, to most Japanese, the American legal system seems a little crazy."

"I'm not going to try to defend the American legal system. Something is definitely broken."

"Why don't Americans fix it?"

"I don't know, exactly. One barrier to reform is that there are too many vested interests protecting the current system, so agreement can't be reached on how to fix it. Some people support radical change and others are fearful they will become victims of unfair changes. It's a difficult problem because the American system is essentially based on idealism. We honestly believe that an individual's life and rights are important. Most of us don't accept arguments that individual rights should be sacrificed. Despite that, we still act in ways that contradict this principle. As a Japanese-American, I'm especially sensitive to this because one hundred twenty thousand Japanese-Americans, most of them U.S. citizens, were rounded up and shipped off to camps in World War II. We weren't treated with the inhuman cruelty of the Nazi concentration camps, but our rights as citizens were certainly trampled. The U.S. Supreme Court said this action was fine, and it took half a century to achieve redress and overturn the legal underpinnings of this action. Most people don't realize that for half a century after World War II, any American president who declared a national emergency could take groups of people selected by race or other criteria and ship them off to a camp with the signing of an executive order."

"Well, the Japanese system may be better, after all."

"I didn't say that. The Japanese system seems to be based on maintaining harmony, not on respecting individuals. It's ironic, but that's exactly the kind of thinking that promoted the camps for Japanese-Americans. Besides, you seem pretty unhappy with the Japanese system."

"Actually, I'm unhappy with Japan."

"Why?"

"We've lost our way. We're drifting without a clear concept of where we should be going as a nation. We adopt Western fads and abandon Japanese customs without any rhyme or reason. Maybe I'm an idealist, too, but we seem to have lost the unique things that make us Japanese."

"Mr. Sugimoto—"

"Call me Buzz. I like people to call me that."

"Okay, Buzz. I don't want to insult you, but I'm puzzled by why you dress the way you do if you have strong feelings about Japan losing her way."

"What do you mean?"

"You dress very much like James Dean."

"Of course. James Dean is a symbol of rebellion and I am still a rebel."

"Yes, but James Dean is an American."

"But he's a Japanese symbol of rebellion. They even feature him in Levi's ads in Japan."

"But Levi's are an American product, too. You're upset about the indiscriminate abandonment of Japanese customs, but you've adopted Western symbols."

Sugimoto looked confused and I thought I had crossed the line between polite chit-chat and what Japanese call "stomach-to-stomach" talk, a frankness that strips away the social straight-jacket that governs so much of Japanese interpersonal relationships. Most stomach-to-stomach conversations occur between old friends or after a great deal of *sake* and beer has been consumed. Sugimoto was drinking beer, but I just had a soft drink and there would be no excuse for me drifting over the line, except that I was an ignorant gaijin.

Fortunately, Sugimoto was taken by the novelty of an observation that was obvious. As is often the case, perhaps it was so obvious that no one had ever mentioned it to him before. We spent the rest of the evening talking about safer topics, like Japanese art and the economy.

IO

We finished the dinner and Sugimoto offered to hail me a cab. By now, I was familiar with the Yamanote line and knew that I could get off at Shimabashi station near the hotel, so I begged off and said my goodnights to him. It was around eleven, the time when most of the nightlife in the city starts to wind down, and it was a pleasant ride back to the station.

I got off and made my way down the platform to the street. In the station, I had taken out my tourist map of Tokyo to make sure I knew where I was going and decided to take a shortcut by following the path of the overhead railway.

Under the tracks of the railway, a whole culture thrives. In every little nook and cranny you'll find small bars, *yakitori* chicken stands, or parking. In a city where you have to prove you have a parking spot before you can buy a car, that latter use for the space under the tracks is especially precious.

Near the station were some small bars tucked into the concrete arches that hold up the elevated tracks. The bars had large lanterns with kanji written on them, probably the name of the bar. I noticed a small mound of salt near the entrance to a couple of them, a Shinto religious invocation. A block past the station, the bars petered out and the arches were used for storage and parking. I was in a dark part of the alleyway with the arches of the railway to my right and to my left, a tall concrete wall.

I was thinking about what I should do the next day. I was interested in taking a trip to Kamakura to see the sights. Kamakura is less than an hour from Tokyo and it's where the giant bronze statue of Buddha is. It's also full of historic shrines and sites from Japan's past. I had a lot of things on my mind except the one thing I would have thought about if I had been in the same situation in Los Angeles or New York: Was I safe?

Someone behind me bumped into a trash can, causing a sudden noise. I turned around to see what the fuss was and saw two men a few feet behind me. If I were a cartoon character, I'd have jumped about five feet in the air. As it was, I think I actually gave a physical start as I realized who was following me. They were the same two men from the previous night.

When they saw that I recognized them, they started coming towards me at a half trot. Scientists say humans have a flight or fight reaction when faced with danger. Maybe Sam Spade would have considered it an evening's sport to duke it out with two thugs in a dark Tokyo alley, but it was no contest for me to choose between fight or flight. I turned and flew.

I could hear them running behind me. Ahead it was just as dark and deserted as the stretch I had come through, and I didn't think I could count on any help. I knew that sooner or later I would come across a street, but I had no idea how far I would have to run. Spurred on by a massive jolt of adrenaline, I was outpacing my two pursuers, but I had no idea where I was going.

Ahead I could see what looked like doors to a shopping arcade under the train tracks. Pale light flooded out from the glass double doors that marked the entrance. I decided to see if any of the shops in the arcade were open. I pushed open the glass doors and ran in. I quickly looked up and down the arcade. It was lined with row upon row of tiny stalls selling souvenirs, electronics goods, and T-shirts. They were all closed, with metal grates pulled down in front of them. I was like a rat trapped in a tunnel.

I thought about trying to get back into the alley, but a glance through the glass doors showed me that the two goons had already caught up with me. I had thrown my lead away. I turned and started running down the central corridor of the arcade, praying that I wasn't going to hit a dead end or locked doors. In the enclosed space of the arcade I could hear the pounding feet of my pursuers, and when I risked a glance over my shoulder, I could see that the taller of the two had pulled ahead and was gaining on me.

I ran for what seemed like blocks before I saw another set of glass doors at the end of the corridor. I wondered if I should slow down and realized that if I did I might be caught from behind. Trusting that the doors were unlocked, I ran up to them and pushed my way through. If they had been locked, the pursuit would have ended with a splat. Fortunately, I was able to surge through them, only slowing down slightly.

I burst onto a cross street that went under the railroad tracks and glanced to the left to see if there were any oncoming cars. That, of course, was a mistake. Since Japan drives on the left side of the road, I should have glanced to the right first and then to the left. Panic and force of habit made me do the reverse.

When I did look to the right, I saw I was about to run into a passing car. It was a convertible with the top down, and unable to stop, I launched myself into the air and landed in the backseat of the vehicle. The driver jammed on the brakes and came to a screeching stop.

I found myself wedged between the front seat and the biggest belly I've ever encountered. With a person this obese you'd expect the stomach to be pillowy and soft, but the belly I landed on was hard as a rock.

"Hey, bruddah, what you think you doin'?" the mountainous backseat passenger said to me. The voice was angry, but it was music to my ears. It was English with a Hawaiian accent.

"Two guys are chasing me," I said excitedly. "Please help me. I'm a Hilo boy." I mentioned my hometown in Hawaii like it was some kind of magic talisman. There was no logic to it, but I figured that telling this enormous man that I was also an island boy might help. It did.

"Hilo?"

"Yes. My house was right by Coconut Island." Coconut Island is a small island in Hilo bay.

"I come from Olaa," the backseat passenger said, the anger draining from his voice. He was acting as if flying Hawaiian tourists landed on his stomach all the time and the natural thing to do was to exchange the name of our hometowns. Olaa is a very small town on the big island of Hawaii, and not too far from Hilo.

Before we could finish our introductions, the doors of the arcade burst open and the two thugs ran out into the street. I lifted my head up to look at them and then I looked at the man I landed on. To my surprise, he was wearing a kimono, and he looked very young. His hair was long and slicked down into a fancy curve on the top of his head. He was a sumo wrestler! His eyes narrowed. "Are these da guys chasin' you?"

"Yeah."

The man grabbed me by the shoulder and leg. He lifted me as easily as you would lift a baby, and he put me down on the seat next to him. Then he stood up. Despite my excitement from the chase and the shock of its abrupt end, I looked with a dropped jaw. The guy was close to seven feet tall and he must have weighed five hundred pounds. He was simply the biggest human I've ever met, and his height was amplified by the fact that he was standing up in the back of a car. It was awesome.

My two pursuers must have agreed, because after a few seconds of stunned shock with their faces tilted upward, they both turned and shot down the street.

A low chuckle started from deep within the enormous belly of my benefactor, and in a few moments, he was laughing uproariously. Watching my erstwhile tormentors, I couldn't help but join in. My two pursuers looked like they could sprint for Japan at the Olympics as they scrambled down the street.

The giant sat down and composed himself. He almost filled the backseat of the car, jamming me up against the side. The driver said something to him in Japanese and he waved the driver on. As we drove along, the *sumotori* asked me, "Why were they chasin' you, bruddah?"

"I honestly don't know. They chased me last night, too, so I don't think it was a random mugging. Tokyo has twelve million people and I don't see how I could come across the same two muggers."

My large companion peered down at me and said, "Say, you look familiar."

"I've been on some TV commercials for a show called *News*

Pop. That's why I'm in Japan. I'm supposed to appear on it in a few days."

The sumotori snapped his fingers. "Dat's it. You're da kine detective."

"I'm not a detective. I just solved a murder."

He smiled. "You better do some detecting on da two punks, bruddah."

Hawaiian Pidgin English has its own vocabulary and grammar. I've forgotten all of mine, but I can still detect the rhythm of Pidgin. He was talking an accented English, not true Pidgin. It's just as well, because I don't know if I could still communicate with a Pidgin speaker. "Who are you?" I asked.

"Gary Apia. Also known as Torayama. Dat's my *shikona,* my sumo fighting name."

"What's an island boy doing in Japanese sumo?"

"There's all kinds of island boys in sumo. Jesse Takamiyama, Konishiki, and Musashimaru are all island boys. Chad Rowan is *Akebono,* he's da *Yokozuna.*"

"What?"

"Chad Rowan fights with the shikona of Akebono. He's da champ. A Yokozuna is a grand champion, da tops in sumo. I'm still in the *Juryo* division. Dat's sort of the minor leagues farm club of sumo. I'll be moving up to the majors soon. That's when da big bucks come, bruddah."

"Well, you're already the champ as far as I'm concerned. If you hadn't come along, I don't know what I'd have done. You said you're from Olaa?"

"Yeah."

"Do you know Henry Tanaka?"

"Sure! I went to high school with his kid, George."

"I'm Henry's cousin, Ken." Hawaii is actually a small place, especially for old-time families. I took Gary to be a Samoan or Tongan and not Hawaiian, so his family might be relatively new to Hawaii. But if he claimed Olaa as home, it was a safe bet that he either knew my cousin or he knew someone who knew him. In Hawaii, even for a bigger city like Hilo, that was always a good bet.

"Dat so? Gee, bruddah, you're a long way from home."

"So are you."

He laughed. "Dat's true. Dat's why we island boys gotta stick together! You need help? You call da *Torabeya* and ask for me. In fact, you can come to da *beya* anytime if you want to see us work out. Jes tell 'em that you're da kine friend of mine. I'm goin'a sumo party right now, but after I get dropped off, I'll have da driver take you anywhere. Jes ask."

"Right now, I'd like to be taken to a police department." Despite what Sugimoto had told me about Japanese cops, I decided it was time to talk to them about my two persistent shadows.

II

Inspector Ishii of the Tokyo police sat back at his cluttered metal desk. "You sure the two men were chasing you?" he asked. His accent was so thick you could pick it up with a chopstick. I had to listen intently to understand him. They called him in especially to deal with me in English, and it took over an hour for him to arrive at the station. I wanted to take my best shot at getting aid from the Tokyo police. Asking him to repeat everything he said to me didn't seem like a good tactic for accomplishing this.

"That's right." The metal chair I was sitting on was hard and uncomfortable.

"How do you know?"

"Inspector, those guys chased me for blocks. They weren't just out for a late night jog. This is the second time they've followed me."

"How did you get away?"

"Yesterday, I lost them on a train. I slipped out as the doors were closing. Tonight, I got the help of a sumo wrestler."

Ishii showed a flicker of interest. Maybe he was a sumo fan. "Which *rikishi*?"

"That's a word I don't know."

"A rikishi is a sumo wrestler."

"Oh. His name was Gary Apia. He wrestles under the name of Torayama."

"Oh, a Juryo rank rikishi." Definitely a fan, but apparently it would have gotten me more help if I had jumped on the belly of a big-name sumo champ. In fact, Ishii seemed irritated by the whole situation. They had probably dragged him from home to take care of an excited English-speaking tourist.

"Could you identify these men?"

"I think so. I've seen them for the past two nights."

Ishii made no comment. He went to a shelf and took down two large books. He put them in front of me and flipped them open. Mug books, with several rows of pictures on each page. "Please look at these pictures. If you see the men, tell me."

I nodded and Ishii left to get himself a cup of tea. The room we were in had no private offices. Instead there was a small area with a couple of plastic-covered couches. The rest of the office was filled with small metal desks jammed together in rows, similar to the television station. Ishii's desk sat at the end facing a row of desks, which probably meant he was a supervisor or section chief for investigators. His business card, which was in Japanese, wasn't much help to me in figuring out the hierarchy. The room was incredibly cluttered, with white boards on the walls with various notes and charts. The floor was linoleum, and although it was old, it was spotless. Uniformed officers were coming in, making jokes, drinking tea, sitting down, and working on reports. They wore a gray military-style uniform.

I started the tedious task of flipping through the books, page by page, looking at the individual photos. After forty minutes I called Ishii back to me and pointed at a picture in the book.

"I'm sure this is one of the men who chased me."

Ishii glanced down at the photo. I noted a look of surprise. "This one?"

"This one. I'm positive. There was another guy with him, quite a bit taller and thinner. I didn't see his picture in these two books."

Ishii went to another section of the squad room and returned with another mug book. "Please look at this book. See if you can identify the other man." This time he stood over my shoulder as I flipped through the book. About a quarter of the way through

I found the guy with the wolfish gait. I looked up at Ishii and said, "That's him."

Ishii sat down. "Could you explain exactly what you're doing in Japan?"

That seemed a peculiar question, but I told him I was appearing on the *News Pop* television show.

"Are you some type of political activist in the United States?"

"No, I'm just here because I got involved in the murder of a Japanese businessman. That's why they want me on *News Pop*."

He looked at me and said, "It's strange."

"What's strange?"

Ishii pointed to the picture of the thin man. "The first books were known thieves and muggers. The man you identified is a thug named Junichi Honda. He has ties to the Yakuza and a variety of radical political groups. This book has pictures of known members of radical groups." He pointed to the second picture I identified. "This is a picture of Kim Chung Hee," he said. "Does that name mean anything to you?"

I looked at him quizzically. I shrugged.

"Early in his career, Kim was a Yakuza, a Japanese Mafia member. Then he became interested in right-wing politics and he joined the *Nippon Tokkotai*."

"Nippon . . . ?"

"Nippon Tokkotai."

"What's that?"

"It means Japanese Special Attack Force."

"Sounds like a military group."

"It's a radical political group. Tokkotai was what they called the *Shimpu* attack forces in the Pacific War. Americans called them *Kamikaze*. Nippon is an old-fashioned word for Japan. It's a very conservative word. Now we usually use Nihon. The Nippon Tokkotai is a right-wing group that wants to restore what they consider Japanese virtues, or *Yamato Damashii*, the Japanese spirit. They don't like the West and want to return to pure Japanese culture."

"They're a right-wing group?"

"Yes. Like in the United States, Japan has both right-wing and left-wing groups. But in Japan the groups on the far right are not just conservatives. They are interested in a militaristic and aggressive Japan, just like before the Pacific War. They don't like Japan's current role in the world, and think we should return to prewar thinking and attitudes. They sometimes use violence to make their point. Right now we have these people crashing cars into government buildings to show their protest over current government policies."

"Isn't Kim a Korean name?"

"Yes. It may seem strange, but many Koreans are involved in radical Japanese right-wing groups. It comes from their involvement with the Yakuza. You're sure you're not active in politics in the United States?"

"Not really. I vote and that's about it. I'm just here in Japan to appear on a television show."

"In your television interview you didn't say anything about the Emperor, did you?"

"I haven't been interviewed yet. That's in a couple of days. I've just been in a promotional spot where I say goran kudasai. The subject of the Emperor hasn't come up during my entire stay in Japan. What does the Emperor have to do with this?"

"Japanese right-wing groups, including the Nippon Tokko-tai, have tried to assassinate politicians who have said negative things about the Emperor or Japan's involvement in the war. If you're not active in politics and you haven't done anything to anger them while you're in Japan, I don't know why they would be after you. Maybe it's a case of mistaken identity."

"The way they've followed me for the past two nights doesn't sound like a mistake to me. You said both men also have Yakuza connections?"

"Yes."

"That could be the link. I recently put the son of the leader of the Sekiguchi-gummi in jail."

"That's one of the biggest crime families in Japan."

"Could they want to take revenge on me for that? Or maybe try to intimidate me into not testifying at the trial back in the States?"

Ishii shrugged. "It's a possibility."

"Are you going to bring the two men in for questioning?"

"What for? They didn't do anything yet. If we brought them in we couldn't hold them. They'll have friends who will swear they were with them at the time you were chased."

"Then I should have let them catch me and beat the hell out of me, or maybe stick a knife in me?"

For the first time, I saw Ishii smile. "That would make a stronger case. If you had witnesses. And they would testify." So much for Sugimoto's stories about the Japanese police acting like that Chinese emperor willing to kill two innocent men to assure that a third guilty party was punished. Ishii wasn't even willing to bring the two guys in for questioning. I guess he figured that in a few days I'd be out of the country and the problem would literally go away.

I took a cab back to the hotel. My walking days in Tokyo were over.

12

It was late when I finally got back to the hotel. I thought of calling Mariko, but it would be early in the morning L.A. time and I didn't want to wake her. Instead, I spent a restless night. When I did sleep I had bad dreams of being chased. It didn't take a psychiatrist to figure out where that came from. Like many Asians, I place great store in dreams, but these dreams were neither illuminating nor prescient. They were simply disturbing. I woke tired the next morning and placed a call to Mariko at the Kawashiri Boutique.

"Kawashiri Boutique." The connection was extremely clear. It was Mrs. Kawashiri.

"Hi, Mrs. Kawashiri. This is Ken. Can I talk to Mariko?"

A hesitation. Then, in a funny tone, "Mariko's not here now."

"Is something wrong, Mrs. Kawashiri?"

"No, no, nothing is wrong. She's just not here now. But nothing is wrong."

"Well, tell her I called. I'll try her at home later."

"She might be out tonight."

I was puzzled. "Are you sure something isn't wrong?"

"No, she just mentioned that she'd be busy tonight. Don't worry, Ken-san. Everything is fine."

"All right. I hope things are going fine for you."

"Oh yes. Thank you for asking."

"Well, I'll see you in a few days."

"Yes. You'll have to tell me about your adventures in Tokyo."

"Don't worry. I'm collecting plenty of adventures to tell. I'll talk to you later. Good-bye."

"Good-bye."

As I was talking to Mrs. Kawashiri the message light on the phone blinked on, indicating that a call came in while I was on the line. I called the message number and an operator with impeccable English told me that Junko had called. I dialed the number the operator gave me and it was picked up on the first ring.

"Junko?"

"Yes."

"This is Ken Tanaka."

"I'm so glad you called right away," Junko said excitedly. "Professor Hirota, the man who wrote the article on Kannemori swords, is back in town and he's very anxious to talk to you and see your sword. I was hoping I could set up a meeting today."

"Those swords are the furthest thing from my mind right now."

"What do you mean?"

"I had an adventure last night. The two guys who chased me the night before chased me again. I'm beginning to think they might be Yakuza intent on taking revenge for the crime I solved in Los Angeles." I explained to her what happened, including my interview with the police. We men are supposed to be strong, silent types, but it made me feel better to talk about what had happened.

"That's very frightening," she said. "You were very lucky that rikishi found you."

"I found him by landing in his lap, but it was a stroke of luck that he was a fellow Hawaiian. Frankly, I'm reluctant to do more sightseeing in Tokyo with the Yakuza after me."

"Let me talk to the producers," Junko said. "I'm almost done with the tape introduction to your segment so you don't have to be in town. Maybe the producers will pay for you to leave Tokyo until the show date. You can go to Nikko or someplace like that."

"I'd feel a lot safer if that was possible. It would also be more fun than sitting in a hotel room for two days."

"Why don't you come down to the studio and we can discuss it," Junko said.

"Okay, but I'm going to take a cab."

When I got to the studio, Junko made me repeat my story in great detail. As I finished, her phone rang. Professor Hirota had arrived. "He must have rushed over," Junko said. "I told you he sounded excited on the phone." Junko and I went to a reception room with four leather chairs arranged around a coffee table to meet the professor.

Professor Hirota was not what I expected. Instead of some musty scholar, bent over and myopic from too many books, I saw a neatly dressed man in his early thirties carrying a Gucci portfolio under his arm, like some eager advertising executive. I stuck out my hand and he shook it. Instead of the soft hands of a scholar, I was surprised to feel the rough hands of a construction worker.

"Yukihiko Hirota," he said. His English had a British accent to it. I've never met a Japanese who spoke British English instead of American English, and that surprised me.

"Ken Tanaka," I responded.

"I'm extremely pleased that Miss Ohara called me," he said, handing me his *meishi*, or business card. "And I have to admit that I'm bloody excited about the possibility that you might have another of the special swords made by Kannemori. I just got back in town and I had to rush over to see it."

"Frankly, I'm excited about it, too. It's something I picked up at a garage sale and I never anticipated that it would be worth anything more than decoration."

"Well, I'm not a sword appraiser," the professor said, "but if you're interested in selling it I can introduce you to several chaps who would be anxious to buy it. The exact price would depend on the condition, but if it's a genuine Kannemori, I'm sure it's worth at least fifteen to twenty thousand dollars, American."

That surprised me. A windfall.

"Is the sword here?" The professor's eyes had a gleam of youthful excitement, like a little boy before Christmas.

"I'll get it," Junko said. "Why don't you two sit down and relax. I'll also get us some tea."

That the professor jumped into business before some of the Japanese social preliminaries were handled was surprising to me, but I had already concluded that Hirota was a rather interesting man. We both sat down in the chairs around the coffee table, with Hirota putting his portfolio on the table.

"Your English has a British tinge to it," I remarked.

"Yes. People often comment on it. I studied comparative history at Cambridge for two years and I picked up the accent there. To tell you the truth, I've made an effort to keep it because it rather enhances my image in academic circles. There's nothing like an English accent to make even the most banal statement sound reasoned and scholarly. It's pulled my chestnuts out of the fire on more than one occasion when I've made a silly ass of myself in front of colleagues at conferences or such where we use English. Instead of branding me as a dunce, the accent causes them to nod sagely, as if I have just made a singularly intelligent statement."

I laughed and he joined in.

"Are you a sword enthusiast?" he asked.

"No, not unless you count samurai movies."

"Oh? Perhaps something like Zatoichi, the blind swordsman movies?"

I was almost insulted. The Zatoichi movies are great fun, but I'm not a kid. "Actually I was thinking of something like Inagaki's samurai trilogy or any of Kurosawa's samurai films. I even consider Ozu's *Uegestu* a samurai movie, although most would classify it as a ghost film."

He gave me a big smile. "You are a samurai enthusiast!"

"No, just an old film enthusiast. Most of the movies I see don't have too many living actors."

Hirota laughed. "Are you staying in Japan for very long?"

"Unfortunately, no. Just a few more days until the *News Pop* television show is on. I'm scheduled to leave Japan right after that."

"That's unfortunate. It would be wonderful if you could see the real Japan, not just the crowding and glitter of Tokyo. I perceive that you are of Japanese ancestry, and it would be wonderful if you could trace down your roots."

"If I ever get to return to Japan that will be a project I'll try to arrange. Right now I'm just trying to stay out of trouble until the television show."

"Well, there are still many things to see in Tokyo. I hope you have a pleasant time in our country."

"It's been eventful, if nothing else, but I hope the rest of my stay will be nice."

Before we could continue Junko came in with a tray holding two covered, handleless cups filled with green tea, the ubiquitous refreshment in Japanese business meetings. She put them down before us and left to get the sword.

"When you said 'eventful' you used a tone that makes me wonder what you meant. Has anything untoward happened during your stay here?"

"Well, I've been chased twice by a couple of Yakuza thugs, not something on the usual tourist itinerary."

"Yakuza? What on earth for?"

"I don't know for sure, but in the case that got me on *News Pop,* I put away the son of the head of the Sekiguchi-gummi. I think they're trying to take revenge."

"That is frightening. I do hope you're taking every precaution to assure your safety."

"I'm going to do what they used to do in the old West. I'm leaving town. I'll return on the day of the show."

"I thought the frontier marshal always stayed in town to fight it out with the tough guys." Hirota picked up his cup to sip the hot tea.

"That was Gary Cooper in *High Noon.* This is Ken Tanaka in Tokyo. I don't feel I have a responsibility to protect the capital city of Japan from a couple of Yakuza. The Tokyo police don't seem too interested in pursuing the case, so I'm going to do what's best to protect me."

"Please do. I'm afraid this will probably leave a very bad impression with you about Japan. Our society seems to break down with each passing day and I'm sorry you've been disappointed by your visit here."

"Not disappointed. It's actually been wonderful. The situation I find myself in is a legacy from Los Angeles, so it's not something the typical tourist would encounter."

Junko returned with the sword in its scabbard. Hirota stood up, his eyes bright with anticipation. "May I inspect it?" he asked me.

"Of course," I said.

He carefully took the sword from Junko and placed it on the coffee table. He unzipped his portfolio and took out a large piece of folded white paper. He unfolded the paper and placed it on the coffee table. It covered the tabletop, overlapping slightly. He moved the sword so it was sitting on the paper. Then he withdrew the sword from its scabbard and placed it down on the paper. He examined it in silence for several moments, then he picked it up and sighted down its blade, with the sharpened side up.

"It's really in marvelous condition," he said. "The scabbard and handle are a bit scruffy, but the blade, which is the soul of the weapon, is still bright and sharp. It certainly looks like a Kannemori sword, but I would have to remove the handle and examine the tang to make sure. I don't know how complete an inspection you'll allow me, but I'd like to, at a minimum, take a rubbing of the blade."

He reached into his portfolio and took out two manila envelopes, each labeled in kanji. He opened them and took out two large pieces of tissue paper. Each piece of paper held the image of a sword blade, done in reddish-brown chalk. The tissue paper was put over the blade and the chalk was rubbed across the sword, transferring the patterns on the blade to the paper. The designs were quite clear. One of the blade rubbings ended at the sword guard, but the other was of the complete blade with the handle and guard removed. The tang of this blade had kanji characters incised in it.

"These are rubbings of two other Kannemori swords with these unusual patterns. This sword is at the Japan National Museum." He indicated the rubbing without a tang and then pointed to the other rubbing. "And this is a Kannemori sword owned by a private collector in Kyoto."

"They're different," I pointed out.

"Yes. The patterns on each are quite distinctive. It's a highly unusual feature for a Japanese sword. You'll note I couldn't get permission to remove the handle of the sword at the Japan National Museum, so I don't have an impression of the tang. I had a request in to the museum to allow me to do this, but the sword was stolen before it was granted."

"Stolen?"

"Yes. A student who was working as an intern at the museum apparently stole the sword. He was only a suspect, but he recently committed suicide, apparently in remorse. They searched his room, but they couldn't find the sword. It's a very tragic case."

"Why is the tang important?"

Hirota pointed to the kanji on the rubbing with a tang. "This is the name of the swordsmith and the date the sword was made. 'Nineteenth year of Keicho,' which is 1614 on the Western calendar."

"Your article said there was also the number three on the tang," Junko said. "Did you get any more information on what that means?"

"Here's the number," Hirota said, pointing at a kanji that looked like three parallel strokes. "I'm afraid the number is as mysterious as when I wrote the article. Frankly, I'm curious to see if Mr. Tanaka's blade also has a number on the tang. I'm prepared to take a rubbing of your blade right now, but actually I'd like to take your sword with me and remove the handle to take a complete rubbing of the tang. I'll take very good care of it, and the sword will be restored to proper condition. In fact, I'll even have the handle restored at my expense, because it looks in need of refurbishment."

"Will you have the sword back by the show?" Junko interjected.

"When is the show?"

"In two days."

"Oh, I'll be done by then," Hirota said. "And I know an expert restorer who I'm sure will restore the handle on a rush basis, if I ask him. I'm positive I can get my work done in two days. So what do you think, Mr. Tanaka? I'll be able to authenticate your sword as a Kannemori, you'll get the handle refurbished, and I'll guarantee that I'll have the sword back in time for the television show. Will you let me take your sword?"

I wanted him to authenticate the sword, but I was a little curious about the blade and wanted more information. Without answering him I asked, "Do you know what the patterns on the blades mean?"

"It's supposed to be some kind of message, although what kind of message I don't know. On your blade there's a mountain with two peaks and what looks like a line of some kind. I don't know what that line means, but the mountains are *yama* in Japanese, so they may be part of two names."

"I met a wrestler named Torayama last night," I said.

"That means Tiger Mountain, a good name for a rikishi," Hirota said. He pointed at one of the rubbings. "On the Kyoto blade there's a rock outcropping that looks like the letter *M* and what appears to be a forest. On the Japan museum blade there are two temples and a stream between them. I've wracked my brain but I don't know what this is all supposed to mean."

"What about the legend?" Junko said. "Your article said something about a legend, but it didn't give any details."

"That's what Sonoda-san says. He's the owner of the Kyoto blade. He says there's a legend associated with the blades and that the patterns on the blade give some kind of instructions. I don't know if that's true, because I've checked the ancient texts and there's no mention of a legend associated with these swords. Sonoda-san says he has a family connection that allowed him to learn of the legend. I could repeat what little I know, but it would be a lot more interesting coming directly from Sonoda-san, who knows all the details. If you're serious about learning more, I could introduce you to Sonoda-san, and I'm sure he'd be happy to tell you what he knows."

"Mr. Sonoda lives in Kyoto?"

"That's right."

I looked at Junko. Getting things from the horse's mouth is always best, but I wasn't sure how I would get to Kyoto. "Instead of Nikko, would the producers pay for me to stay in Kyoto until the show?"

"I'm sure they would. It actually might be easier to stay out of trouble in a big city like Kyoto, instead of a small town like Nikko."

I turned to Hirota. "Dr. Hirota, you are welcome to examine my blade as fully as you wish. I'd like a couple of things, though. One is a copy of whatever rubbing you make of my blade. I can frame it and it will make a nice keepsake if I ever sell the sword. I'd also like photocopies of the other two rubbings you have."

Hirota looked surprised. "What on earth for?"

"In addition to the Japan National Museum theft, two other Kannemori swords were stolen recently, one in New York and one in Rotterdam. That makes three swords by an ancient Japanese swordsmith stolen in a short amount of time."

"How do you know that?"

"Junko uncovered it while doing computer research for the show."

"So Kannemori blades are being stolen?"

"That's correct."

"Which means . . ." Hirota raised his eyebrows, clearly intrigued.

I laughed. "I don't know what it means. I'm just curious and lately I've been making a hobby of satisfying my curiosity."

Junko made the photocopies of Hirota's rubbings for me, reducing them to a sheet of paper that was approximately legal size. Hirota promised to contact Mr. Sonoda in Kyoto to arrange a meeting and he said he'd tell Junko about it.

When our business was done Hirota left, clutching my sword. Junko looked at me as soon as Hirota left the meeting area and said, "What do you have in mind about those swords?"

I sighed. "Do you have hunches in Japan?"

"Hunch?" It was the first time I had stumped her with an English word.

"A feeling. Intuition. The thought that something might be important, even though you don't have all the facts to prove that thought is true."

"Oh yes, *chokkan*. We have that," Junko said.

"Well, I've got a hunch about these swords. It's strange that, in a few weeks' time, several examples of the work of some obscure seventeenth-century swordmaker should get stolen. I believe in coincidence, but if this is only a coincidence, it's a very strange one. I just want to gather some information about these swords to see if there's a pattern."

"So you're starting to work on another mystery while you're here in Japan?" Junko asked, rather excited.

I laughed. "I don't know what I'm doing, except satisfying my curiosity. I don't know if there is a mystery. In mystery books and detective movies all sorts of things fit together to form a complicated plot, but in life things just happen. Sometimes they're connected and sometimes they're not."

Sugimoto stuck his head in the room and nodded to me. "Sorry to hear about last night," he said. "I should have gone with you to the hotel to make sure you'd be safe."

"Don't be silly," I said. "No real harm was done, and I got to see the inside of a Tokyo police station."

"Can you excuse us for a minute while we talk Japanese?" Sugimoto said.

"Sure."

He started talking to Junko and both their demeanors changed radically with the switch in language. He became very abrupt during his conversation and Junko became very submissive, even bowing her head at the end of the conversation. It surprised me to see the transformation, and although my meager Japanese wouldn't allow me to keep up with the conversation, I heard Sugimoto say *baka,* or fool, several times. When he was done he looked at me and said, "Sorry to interrupt your conversation," and left abruptly.

"What was that all about?" I asked Junko.

"He thinks I'm wasting time on this sword business and ordered me to stop. I apologized for upsetting him."

"Have I gotten you in trouble?"

"No. Japanese males think they can order any female around. I didn't want to argue, so I nodded meekly and agreed with him. Now he's going away happy and I can continue doing what I want to. That's how we females handle things here. I have what you call a hunch, too. My hunch is that this might turn into a terrific story, and I want to help you get more information about the swords before the show. Sugimoto-san may think it's stupid, but if it doesn't turn out to be a good story we won't lose too much."

"How are you going to help?"

"I'll make sure Hirota-san sets up a meeting for you with Sonoda-san in Kyoto. I'll also make sure the producers pay for your trip. I'll make the arrangements so you can leave tomorrow morning. I've also got some other ideas that I want to check on."

"That sounds great. I hope this doesn't cause conflict for you with Sugimoto-san."

"Sugimoto-san doesn't accept it, but for now we're equals on the show. He can't tell me what to do. With his connections he'll be far above me someday, but right now he can't really do anything to me."

"He's got connections?"

"Oh, yes. His family is very rich. His father owns a record business and the family bought a lot of Tokyo real estate in the sixties. The real estate market isn't what it used to be, but Sugimoto-san's family got into it early enough so they weren't too hurt when the market deflated. Buzz-san is in television because he thinks he's making it on his own, but his family's money and influence have opened a lot of doors for him."

"But he told me he's a rebel. I didn't see him as a member of an establishment family."

Junko laughed. "He's just old for being a rebel. A lot of Japanese males go through a stage of rebellion before they settle into a corporate life as a salaryman. Usually it's in college, but Buzz-san has just clung to that role longer than most."

"A salaryman is an office worker?"

"I guess you would call them a company man in English. Buzz-san will stop wearing the Levi's and T-shirts some day and slip into a dark suit and tie. Then his family connections will shoot him to the top, and he knows it. That's why he's so conservative. Did he talk to you about the decline of Japan yet?"

"Just briefly at dinner last night."

"It's one of his favorite subjects. Don't let the clothes fool you. In his heart he's still a fiercely traditional Japanese male."

"Junko, did you tell Buzz about my encounter with the two thugs last night?"

"No. Why?"

"No reason," I answered vaguely.

I took a cab back to the hotel. I wasn't willing to test my fleet-
ness of foot against the Yakuza again. I had lunch and dinner
brought up to my room and spent most of the day watching
Japanese television. I watched a baseball game that ended in a 3–3
tie, and that puzzled me. In the U.S. the teams would play until
one or the other got ahead, but in Japan a tie seemed perfectly
acceptable. About an hour after dinner there was a knock on my
door.

"Who is it?"

"Hotel masseuse." A female voice, with impeccable English.
I was immediately wary.

"I didn't order a massage," I said.

"It's the chambermaid."

I was surprised by the change in identification.

"Who is it?" I asked.

"Candygram."

I knew that voice, but I couldn't believe it was true. I opened
the door to a grinning Mariko. "What are you doing here?" I
spluttered.

"Aren't you glad to see me?" she said. "Are you going to in-
vite a girl in, or what? I'm dying for a shower."

I rushed out and hugged her, giving her a big wet kiss. Instead
of just inviting her in, I practically carried her into the room.

"Now that's a proper greeting!" she said.

"But I still can't figure out what you're doing here."

"Well, I missed you."

"But, but . . ."

"Mary and I had dinner right after you left, and I was already feeling kind of blue. She asked me why I didn't go with you. I didn't have a good answer except money, so she offered to lend me the money. She said I should go to Japan. When I asked her when, she said tomorrow. I thought she was kidding but she was entirely serious. Apparently she does this all the time, and she was able to finagle tickets at a good price. It seemed like a tremendous adventure, my passport was current, and my credit card almost paid off, so I jumped on a plane and here I am."

"You borrowed the money from Mary?"

"Of course not."

"But I'm leaving in four days."

She looked at me archly. "Boy, just because I fly across the Pacific Ocean to surprise you, you mustn't think I'm going to tag along like a puppy dog. When you leave I'm going to hole up in one of those cheap businessmen's hotels. I intend to stay ten days or two weeks or whenever I max out my credit card, whichever comes first. You're going back to L.A. and I'm going to be loose in Japan once you leave. I thought it was a great chance to be here with you for some time and to still see something of the country. Do you mind having me as a roommate for a few days? If you do, I can check into a hotel now."

"Mind? I'd love it! But how did you get the money for the ticket?" As a struggling actress, Mariko did not have a lot of cash lying around.

She sighed. "To tell you the truth I got the money by doing something I swore I'd never do again."

"You don't mean . . ."

"Yes."

"But you said it was too humiliating to do again."

"I know. But I didn't see any other way to get some money quickly." She sighed. "I asked my parents for a loan. That means at least a couple of years of flying back to Columbus to see them for major holidays, and it might even mean having them come to California for a visit. If I knew a loan shark that would lend me the money I'd have gone to him. I'd rather have broken kneecaps than my mother lecturing me about giving up acting, getting married again, and having nice, fat, little Japanese grandchildren for her."

"I know what a sacrifice it is, but I'm glad you did it. I can't believe you're here."

"Neither can I."

"I called Mrs. Kawashiri this morning and she acted cagey when I asked for you. I guess you were already in the air and she didn't want to spoil the surprise."

"She was super about letting me take time off on short notice."

"You better buy her a nice gift."

"You're pretty free with my money. Or rather my parent's money."

I shook my finger at her in mock admonishment. "I know your parents raised you right. You may have been just about the only Japanese girl in Columbus, Ohio, but you still know what to do when someone has been as nice to you as Mrs. Kawashiri."

She raised her eyebrow. "Gee, I didn't think that lecturing me would be what you'd do once you got over your surprise."

Well, I know a cue when I hear one. I took Mariko in my arms and tried to do my best to satisfy her expectations. They say absence makes the heart grow fonder, but so does abstinence. I know I'm over forty and I also know we were apart for only a few days, but there's a great secret they don't write about in detective novels: Successfully eluding crooks is an exhilarating shot to the libido. I had eluded my two friends two nights in a row and frankly I felt pretty frisky.

When Mariko and I were back to a state where we could communicate in full sentences, I said, "I almost forgot. I'm leaving for Kyoto tomorrow morning."

"What? Why?"

"For my health."

Mariko looked puzzled.

"I called you this morning to tell you about another encounter I've had with the same two guys who chased me. The police say they're Yakuza. I've decided it isn't safe to be in Tokyo, so the television show is paying to get me out of town. While I'm in Kyoto, I'm also going to talk to a sword collector about that sword I bought in the garage sale."

"So you're actually leaving tomorrow morning?"

"That's right."

"You won't get away from me that easily. I'm going to Kyoto, too."

"Really?"

"As long as my credit card holds out I might as well see Kyoto as well as Tokyo. If I can go to Japan on a moment's notice, going to another city is a snap."

The phone rang. Mariko kissed me on the cheek and said, "Go ahead and answer it. It might be important. I want to jump into the shower anyway. Oh, and maybe you can call down and have my bags sent up to the room. I checked them with the bell captain."

I picked up the receiver. "Hello?"

"Ken-san?"

"Yes."

"It's Junko. I've got your tickets and information about accommodations in Kyoto for you. I've also got some new information about the swords. I'm in the lobby. Can I come up?"

I glanced at the bathroom door and said hastily, "I'll come down and meet you. There's a bar in the lobby. I'll see you there."

I scrambled into some clothes and stuck my head into the bathroom where Mariko was just stepping out of the shower, a towel wrapped around her head. "There's someone from the television show here. I'm going to meet her in the lobby. Want to come?"

"Sure. Just give me a minute to get on my clothes and fix my hair."

Mariko was true to her word, and it only was a few minutes before we were going down in the elevator. In the lobby bar of the Imperial, Junko was sitting at a table sipping a drink. She saw us and she got a quizzical look on her face.

"This is my girlfriend, Mariko Kosaka," I told Junko as we sat down. "She flew in this evening from Los Angeles to surprise me. If it's possible, she'd like to get tickets to go to Kyoto with me tomorrow."

Junko looked a bit flustered, but she assured me that there would be no problem getting an extra train ticket in the morning.

"You said you had more information about the swords," I reminded her.

"Oh yes." She took some papers out of her purse and handed them to me. They were two faxes. One looked like a page from an auction catalog. It showed a Japanese samurai sword, with the markings on the blade just barely visible. The other page looked like a museum brochure of some kind, but the writing was in Dutch or German. There was a small picture of a samurai sword on this page, along with a drawing of an old sailing ship of some sort. The sword was the bare blade, without the handle.

"The auction catalog is the New York blade. It's not a very good picture, but you can just make out the design on the blade. The other fax is from the Dutch Shipping Museum in Rotterdam. The sword picture on that one is pretty poor quality, but it was the best they were able to come up with. I thought these might help you," Junko said.

I looked at the two faxes closely, but the images were too muddled to really tell me anything. Still, it was better than nothing and I thanked Junko profusely for her efforts. The three of us sat in the bar for about half an hour discussing the arrangements in Kyoto. Mariko, who is a recovering alcoholic, sipped an orange juice and I did the same. I didn't like meeting in the bar because it was unfair to Mariko, but I didn't want Junko up in my room with the bed mussed up the way it was. Despite being a child of the swinging sixties, I'm modest.

When we were done with our discussion, Junko said goodbye and Mariko and I went to the elevator to return to my room. When the doors of the elevator closed, Mariko said, "It's just as well that I came to Japan."

"Why?"

"I think Junko might be a little interested in you."

14

The blue-and-white bullet train slid into the station like a slinking beast. Junko, Mariko, and I were standing on the platform. Mariko and I had baggage in hand. When the train stopped, the doors slid open and we walked into the car.

The interior of the train was off-white and gray with polished aluminum strips framing the windows. The bench seats had a bright blue upholstery, and over the seats was a luggage rack of polished tubular aluminum. Mariko and I found a seat and slung our luggage on the overhead racks.

"How long will the train stop?" I asked.

"Only a few minutes," Junko said. "I'd better say good-bye now. Have fun in Kyoto, and remember that a car and guide will meet you when you arrive. The dinner with Mr. Sonoda is all arranged. I'll see you in two days for the program." Junko shook my hand, then said to Mariko, "It was nice meeting you." Then she left us to return to the platform.

"She's interested in you, all right," Mariko said. "I've got frostbite from that send-off."

"Don't be silly," I said. I feigned indifference, but secretly I hoped Mariko was right. I was very happy with Mariko and had no intention of being unfaithful to her, but let's face it, nothing is as great for the ego as someone finding you desirable.

In under five minutes the train started moving. The doors closed and the car shuddered slightly as the train left the station.

I marveled at how smooth and quiet the train was. Much smoother and quieter than any train in the U.S. I've ever been on.

"How fast do you think we'll be going?" Mariko asked.

"We're on the *Nozomi* train, which is supposed to be the super express. The guidebooks say we'll do a hundred eighty or ninety kilometers per hour. If it's a clear day we should be able to see Mount Fuji on the trip."

Mariko was dressed in black slacks, a dark green turtleneck sweater, and a green jacket. The slim line of the slacks fitted her trim body and made her look much taller than she really was. I had jeans, a shirt, and a ski parka on.

"How long will it take us?"

"A little more than two hours."

As we passed through Tokyo, I could see the density of the buildings gradually thinning until houses started having small yards in the back. These houses had little vegetable gardens and weren't as tightly packed as the buildings in the city, but they were still crowded by American standards. As we reached the outskirts of Tokyo, we could see Mount Fuji in the distant haze, looking like a painted white cone on pale gray silk. In the old days Mount Fuji could be seen from Tokyo almost every day, but smog and smoke now make Fuji a rare sight from the city.

Soon the houses gave way to farmland. The farms were densely cultivated plots in a patchwork quilt. All the plots of land were small and most were flooded with water. Rice paddies. I could see a cluster of houses that formed a small village tucked into the folds of a foothill. On the hill, near a grove of trees, were Buddhist and Shinto headstones that marked a cemetery. The farmland looked very picturesque, and except for the occasional TV antenna or pickup truck, I imagine you could find hundred-year-old woodblock prints that depicted a landscape similar to the one out the window.

When we arrived in Kyoto there was a limo with an English-speaking driver waiting to take us to our hotel. I could get used to this television lifestyle.

That afternoon the driver took us to the Kyoto Gosho, the old Imperial Palace from the days when Kyoto used to be the capital of Japan. Afterwards we were taken to a craft center where we looked at pottery and woodblock prints. I love Japanese woodblock prints, but the high prices kept us from buying, except for a rather nice vase that Mariko said was for Mrs. Kawashiri.

The next day we were taken to a bewildering succession of temples and shrines. Kyoto has over sixteen hundred temples, and our driver seemed determined to show us all of them. He was an affable man in his late thirties. Despite his smile, the rest of his face had a strained look, as if we were always behind some unstated timetable. When he drove he hunched over the wheel like Mickey Rooney in the camp autoracing movie, *The Big Wheel,* but, despite his intense posture, he didn't speed. Of the numerous temples we were shown, only Kinkaku-ji, the Golden Pavilion, was memorable, and most of the others sort of blurred into my memory until we got to Ryoanji.

The garden at Ryoanji is a rectangular expanse of white sand fenced on two sides by an austere plaster wall. A verandah made of natural wood borders the other two sides of the garden. The wood of the verandah has been polished to a hard, gleaming brown by uncounted stocking feet gliding across its surface.

In the center of the sand stand fifteen rocks protruding upward. The rocks were set so you couldn't see all of them no matter what your viewing angle was. Small bits of moss clung to the base of most of the rocks. The sand between the rocks was carefully raked to form wavelike patterns that sinuously wound their way around the rocks and throughout the expanse of the garden.

"Ryoanji was first made in the fifteenth century." Mariko was reading from a brochure we got when we entered. "It's famous because of its connection with Zen Buddhism."

As she spoke, a milling and noisy crowd passed us. Children were talking and running about. Japanese tourists stopped, looked, and having seen the famous site, moved on. More than a few were fulfilling the stereotype by furiously snapping photographs. I noticed that in the corner of the verandah an old Japanese couple was kneeling on their heels and staring at the garden. Despite the flow of tourists around them, the sound of voices and the movement, the old man and woman seemed focused on the garden. A marvelous tranquillity was washed across their faces as they sat absorbing each nuance of beauty found in the austerity of the sand, rocks, and moss.

I was in stocking feet like the rest of the tourists. I walked to the edge of the verandah and sank down. I couldn't sit on my heels like the old couple, so I sat cross-legged and stared out across the garden.

The vista reminded me of aerial photographs I've seen of the South Pacific. To me, the rocks and moss seemed like islands set in a swirling white sea. That white sea washed away my anxieties and tension. It was wonderful. My family has been in Hawaii since 1896, and I wondered if the suggestion of islands in the garden was what I really found restful. For some reason this made me feel very disconnected. I wondered if Japan, Hawaii, or California was my spiritual home.

Mariko stood shuffling from foot to foot, already bored and anxious to move on, but she remained silent as I contemplated the garden. After about ten minutes, I turned to her and smiled, then stood up. We left the old couple still seated on the edge of the verandah, looking across the garden in unmoving silence.

When we got back to the car the driver already had the door open, ready to whisk us away to another temple. We got in and I asked Mariko for the brochure on Ryoanji she had picked up. The car swayed slightly as it made its way towards the next temple and it was very peaceful feeling the warmth of Mariko's body next to mine as I read the brochure.

Detecting was the furthest thing from my mind when I turned over the brochure and noticed that it had a stylized map showing where Ryoanji temple was in relationship to other famous places in Kyoto. Mount Uryu-yama and Mount Kazan were shown to the west of the city as stylized icons, and the downtown was marked by an icon of the Kyoto Gosho palace. The Kamogawa river cut its way through Kyoto, and it was shown as a blue ribbon. The Golden Pavilion got its own icon, and Ryoanji was shown as a simple rectangle with tiny rocks in the middle. The folds of the brochure cut the map into neat sections. As I looked at the map I had a kind of Zen epiphany. My mind was clear and not consciously working, but an answer came to me as if in a dream.

"It's not a message. It's a map," I told Mariko.

"What are you talking about?"

"When I talked to that professor, Hirota, he told me that he thought the patterns on the blades were some kind of message. He writes in pictographs, so it's natural for him to think of icons as words. But the patterns are really stylized representations of temples and mountains. There's something else that's like a long line that I haven't figured out, but the rest is now very clear to me. They're all landmarks that would be used in a map. The blades fit together in sections, just like the sections formed by the folds of this brochure."

"But why would you put a map on different sword blades and what is it a map to?"

"I don't know yet. Maybe we should turn around and return to Ryoanji temple and it will come to me."

I was only half joking.

The dinner with Mr. Sonoda had been arranged by Junko, so I didn't know too much when Mariko asked me about where we were going. The driver, our frenetic tour guide of the day, told us that we going to the *Kori-Mizu* restaurant. When I asked him about the restaurant, all he was able to tell me was they served traditional Japanese food and that the name of the restaurant meant ice water, which I thought was a strange name.

The Kori-Mizu was nestled in the hills above Kyoto and the driver took a winding road to get us to it. The car pulled up to a *Torii*-style gate and let us out. Stone steps led up a mountainside, and at the top of a steep stairway we could see the restaurant. Tall trees lined the pathway so it was hard to get a good view of what the restaurant looked like, but it appeared to be very much like a traditional Japanese temple, built of wood and up on pilings, with thick pillars and a gently curved roof line.

The path was illuminated by old-fashioned paper lanterns with candles in them. The flickering candles gave a soft warm yellow glow. The light was further diffused as it bled its way through the thin paper of the lanterns. Despite the steep climb ahead of us, it was actually a very inviting sight to look up the mountainside and see the contrast of the lighted paper lanterns, the illuminated stone stairway, and the dark trees.

Mariko and I made our way up to the restaurant door, where we were greeted by a young lady in traditional Japanese kimono.

The kimono was a thick brocade of white blending into green, with embroidered gold leaves forming a pattern that looked like maple leaves being scattered in a fall wind. We gave our name and the woman bowed deeply. She pointed out cushions where we could sit and remove our shoes. Once we had done so, she provided us with slippers. They were thin plastic slippers that had terry cloth for soles.

I saw that the floor was a light polished wood done in a semi-gloss finish and absolutely flawless in the way it was put together. All the wooden joinery was done with hard crisp lines and there seemed to be no filler used to cover up the inevitable cracks between boards that you'd find in a Western hardwood floor. In its own way it was a work of art and it almost seemed a shame to walk across it, even in terry-soled slippers.

The woman took us down a central corridor. Off to the right and left were individual rooms with shóji screen walls. A few screens were open and we could see small rooms with tatami mats covering the floor and low-set tables. In every room there seemed to be an *ikebana* flower arrangement, pottery, or some painted scroll hanging on the wall. In its austerity, simplicity, and beauty, it was traditionally Japanese.

We came to a place where the building simply divided in two. The wooden hall ended in a platform and was picked up about four feet away. Between the two sections of the building was a tiny wooden bridge. The woman took us across the bridge and I looked down and noticed that a swiftly flowing mountain stream was cutting through the middle of the restaurant. The water from the stream lapped the rocks just a few inches from the edge of the floor. I looked over at Mariko to see if she noticed this unusual architectural feature and I could see that she was both surprised and entranced by it.

The second portion of the building seemed very much like the first. The long central corridor had more rooms leading off each side of it. The woman led us to one of the shóji-screened doors. She dropped to her knees and gave us a short bow. Then she slid the screen back and invited us into the room with a delicate wave of her hand.

Mariko and I walked into the room. Sitting on the floor before the low table was an old Japanese man with a jolly round face and a shock of white hair bursting from the top of his head like a tiny fountain. He was wearing a white shirt and tan pants and was sitting on a purple *zabuton,* or cushion. He was drinking beer from a tiny glass, and on the table before him was an enormous bottle of beer at least eighteen inches high.

"Come in, come in," he said in passable English.

"I hope we're not too late," I said.

"Oh, no, you're right on time."

"I assume you're Mr. Sonoda," I responded. "My name is Ken Tanaka. This is my companion, Mariko Kosaka."

"Of course, Tanaka-san and Kosaka-san, please sit down. May I get you something to drink? A beer? Some sake? Something like that?"

"Maybe just some tea," I said.

"The same for me," Mariko echoed.

"What, don't you drink?"

"I don't drink at all," Mariko said.

"And I rarely drink."

"Young people who don't drink. What's this world coming to?"

I looked at Mariko, a bit concerned that she was going to launch in to a discussion of AA and the reason she doesn't drink, but instead she just gave a small smile and sat down on a zabuton. I followed suit.

The man said something in Japanese to the woman at the door, who put her hands before her and bowed, then slid the door closed. "I asked her to bring you some tea," he said. "Then I asked her to start the first course. I hope you're hungry. I know I've been looking forward to this."

"What are we having?" I asked.

"A pretty traditional Japanese dinner, with some unusual specialties that this restaurant is known for. Actually, the first course will be cold noodles that we dip into a flavored broth. That's normally a dish we only eat in the summer and typically this restaurant wouldn't be serving it this late in the season, but because you are visitors to Kyoto I thought you might be interested in seeing how they serve it here."

How many ways can you serve noodles? I don't know, but I couldn't imagine how serving noodles could be a tourist attraction. The door slid open again; it was the young lady again kneeling before the door. This time she had a tray with a simple but beautiful brown teapot and two cups on it. She put the tray down by the table and put the cups before Mariko and me.

They were brown earthen cups, obviously hand-turned. Each was different and each was intended to be a work of art. The teapot was placed on the table, and with another bow to us, the young lady poured the tea. Then she repeated the entire ritual of leaving the room, getting down, bowing, and closing the door.

"Will she do that all night?" Mariko asked.

"Oh yes, it's an old traditional way of service, but I like old traditional things," Mr. Sonoda said.

"I once worked at a Japanese restaurant in the States," Mariko said, "but I don't know if I could stand an entire evening of that routine. She must do a lot of kneeling, bending, and bowing throughout the course of an evening."

"Yes, she does. She'll be helped by others as our meal is served, but I thought it would be fun for you to see this kind of dinner."

"I'm sure it will be a great experience," I responded. "Your English is pretty good."

"I spent twelve years in the United States."

"On business or in school?"

He laughed. "I went to school long before it was popular for Japanese to go to the United States to get an education. No, I was there on business in the sixties and seventies. I was sent there by the company I used to work for, which was Nissan."

"Is that so?"

"Oh, yes. That's one reason I was anxious to meet and help you. Nissan is a sponsor for *News Pop,* and even though I don't work for Nissan anymore, it's sort of Japanese loyalty to help you out just because of that connection. I'd be anxious to meet you anyway, because I understand you have one of the Kannemori blades, and that's a subject that's fascinated me since childhood."

"If you were in the United States in the sixties, you must have been there just when Japanese car companies were starting out."

"Oh, yes," he said. "Absolutely when they were starting out. In fact, I was there when we didn't know anything about the U.S. market. When we first got into the U.S. market, we opened up an office in Gardena, California, on Alondra Boulevard. For a long time that was the national headquarters for Nissan as well as the Southern California sales office.

"As you might know, in Japan we sell cars door-to-door. When someone comes to the door who is interested in buying a car, we arrange a test drive and take things from there. We were so naive about the U.S. market that we actually tried to sell cars door-to-door in Gardena. We realized that Gardena had more Japanese per square mile than any other city in the United States, so we thought it would be a perfect place to launch a Japanese car. Were we wrong.

"First, they don't sell cars door-to-door in the United States, so when we went around a neighborhood knocking on doors, asking people if they wanted to buy a new car, they thought we were crazy. More important, the fact that there were a lot of Japanese in Gardena actually worked against us. Most of those Japanese had been in the American camps in World War II. Instead of blaming the American government for putting them in the camps, a lot of them were just as mad at Japan for starting the war. They didn't want to have anything to do with a Japanese car. In almost a year of trying, we never did sell a single car door-to-door. Although a lot of Japanese-Americans eventually did buy our automobiles, the foundation of our success was making products that all Americans wanted to buy, not just Japanese-Americans."

The door slid open and this time there were two young ladies, the one who brought us the tea and a second one. Instead of being dressed in a kimono, the second woman was dressed in what I'd call a Japanese farmer's outfit, with a big-sleeved jacket cinched at the waist with a cloth belt and what looked like wraparound pants. In front of them were two straw baskets. One was empty, with a long pair of bamboo chopsticks folded across the top. The other had a large pile of long white noodles in it.

"You might want to see this," Sonoda-san said, getting up from the table. As he did so, the young woman in the Japanese farmer's outfit picked up the basket of noodles and started off down the hall towards the center of the building at a rapid pace. This action puzzled me and I looked to Sonoda for guidance.

"She's going to leave the restaurant and run up the mountain with that basket of noodles," he said.

The woman in the kimono picked up her basket and chopsticks and started down the hall with Mariko, Sonoda-san, and me in tow. She got to the center of the restaurant and took a strip of white cloth from the large sleeve of her kimono. She put one end in her teeth, then she quickly wrapped the cloth around her shoulders. Releasing the end from her teeth, she tied it tight. The effect was to pull up the sleeves of her kimono and expose her arms. I've seen the same maneuver in Japanese samurai movies, where they get the long sleeves of the kimono out of the way before they engage in a sword fight.

She went over to the edge of the platform to the gap that divided the two halves of the restaurant and sunk to her knees. She arranged the empty basket next to her and picked up the long chopsticks. Then she stared down into the stream intently. Sonoda-san explained.

"The young woman who went up the mountainside will take the noodles and throw them into the stream in batches. The stream is spring fed and it's always extremely cold. In fact, when snow runoff feeds the stream it's absolutely icy. As the noodles come down the mountain in the stream, they'll not only get washed, they'll also be chilled. This young lady is going to pluck them out of the stream with chopsticks, and then we'll go back to the room and eat them with a dipping sauce."

"You're kidding."

Mr. Sonoda smiled. "Just watch."

What followed was exactly as he described it. Batches of noodles came down the stream and, with an expert hand, the young woman dipped in her chopsticks and fished out the clumps of noodles from the swiftly flowing water. She put the noodles into her basket. The light from the verandah illuminated the stream and I watched very carefully, but only a few noodles escaped her expert ability to pluck them out of the icy water. It was a spectacularly decadent way to end up with a basket of cold noodles.

When the basket was full, the woman stood up and led us back to our room. She served us each a portion of the still cold noodles and gave us a tiny bowl with a sweet soy-flavored dipping sauce that had green onions in it. They were delicious and the show was an extra attraction.

"Did you spend all your time in Los Angeles?" I asked Mr. Sonoda. He slurped his noodles, Japanese style, making a great deal of noise as he ate them. I've never been able to do that, but to my surprise Mariko was able to pick up the slurping routine rather quickly. She doesn't do that when we eat noodles in Los Angeles.

"Mostly. I loved it in Los Angeles, but the place I love most in the world is Kyoto. I'm glad I was in a position to retire here when my working days were over. Now I follow my interests, especially collecting old Japanese swords."

We finished our noodle course and the shōji screen slid open and the next course was ready to be served. I don't know how the waitress knew we had finished. I looked around to see if there was a camera or a window or somewhere she could be observing us, but there was none. Yet somehow she knew the exact time to serve the next course.

She came into the room and starting putting oval-shaped plates before us. I got mine first, then Sonoda-san, then Mariko. On each plate was a smooth round river rock. Sitting upright on the plate was a grilled fish, complete with scales, head, and tail. The fish was sort of bent in an S shape so that it looked like it was swimming upstream towards the rock.

I didn't know what to do, but wasn't about to ask. All sorts of studies have been done about why men don't ask for directions when they're lost on the road. Many of these studies are very scholarly and erudite, but I think the basic reason is that we're stupid.

I looked at the fish, puzzled for a second, then I picked it up with my chopsticks and bit the head of the fish off. Japanese have some fish snacks where they eat an entire fish: head, tail, scales, and all. Unfortunately, this was not one of them.

Mariko, being a woman and much more sensible than me, asked Sonoda-san, "How do you eat this thing?"

Sonoda-san said, "It's very simple." He demonstrated. "You flip the fish on its side, hold the head down with one chopstick, and use the other chopstick to peel off the fillet." He did exactly as he said, stripping off the fillet with one expert swift motion. "Then you eat the flesh with your chopsticks, avoiding the bones and the scales."

As he finished his explanation there was a lull in the conversation and the only sound that could be heard in the room was the crunch, crunch, crunch of me chewing on the head of a fish. Sonoda-san looked over at me in surprise, then he looked down. There, on my plate, was half a fish. The head was bitten off and the insides of the fish, which had not been cleaned, were sort of spilling out on the plate.

In a traditional restaurant in Japan you may get to use slippers and fancy teacups and chopsticks made of beautifully polished wood, but what you don't normally get is a napkin. So there I sat with a half-chewed fish head in my mouth, trying to figure out how I was going to get out of this situation gracefully. Of course, the answer to that is there was no way to get out of this situation gracefully.

Mariko, seeing my condition, reached in her pocket and came out with a couple of tissues. She handed them to me like a mother dealing with a child and I was able to spit the fish head out into the tissues. During my entire performance, Sonoda-san sat there transfixed, watching me totally frozen. When I was finally able to spit the fish head out, I looked up at him and sort of shrugged. That opened the floodgates.

First a few explosive snickers seemed to escape from him in short gasps. I think he was trying to be polite and not laugh at me, but I could tell it was a losing effort. The snickers started coming out with increasing frequency until finally his face exploded in gales of laughter. I looked over at Mariko and she was laughing. I looked over my shoulder at the waitress, who had not yet left the room, and she was laughing, too. After considering all my options, I did the single thing left for me to do. I started laughing, too.

The fact that I was laughing seemed to set Sonoda-san off even more. He started laughing so heartily that he was rocking back and forth on his cushion. Finally he literally toppled backwards off the cushion, flopping back on the tatami mat and dissolving into a fit of merriment. The laughter would seem to die down periodically, only to flare up again when we heard one of the other people in the room laughing. In the end, we all had tears in our eyes and our sides were actually aching.

As soon as she was able to compose herself, the waitress put her hands before her and bowed very deeply, actually putting her forehead to the mat. She murmured something to me and I could tell it was an apology for laughing at me. She left the room, closing the door behind her. My assumption was that she wanted to hotfoot it down the hallway to the kitchen to tell the rest of the staff about what the crazy gaijin had done.

"I picked this restaurant to show you some unique dishes," Mr. Sonoda said to me, "But I have to admit that I am now the pupil and you are the master in terms of teaching me about unusual ways of eating." That set the three of us off again.

When our giddiness over my fish-eating antics subsided, I thought it would be a good time to get down to business. "Can you tell me about the swords?" I asked.

"Ah, the Toyotomi blades."

"What's that?"

"Those are the swords that you're so interested in. Do you know who the Toyotomi were?"

"No."

"Do you know who Hideyoshi was?"

"Wasn't he the person who united Japan right before Ieyasu Tokugawa established the Shogunate?"

"Very good. Most Americans wouldn't know that. Hideyoshi was a peasant who worked his way up to general while he was a vassal of Nobunaga. That would be hard even today, but it is a measure of his brilliance that he was able to do it when birth and family meant almost everything in Japan.

"Nobunaga was a feudal lord who tried to unite Japan in the late fifteen hundreds by killing his enemies. He was very good at killing, so he came close to his goal of unifying the country. Unfortunately, when you act like that you also make new enemies and Nobunaga was killed by one of his own subordinates before he could finish the job of uniting Japan. There was a scramble for power and several generals, including Ieyasu Tokugawa and Hideyoshi, rushed to take power. Hideyoshi managed to come out on top. The Toyotomi was the clan that Hideyoshi belonged to.

"Hideyoshi was a brilliant general, so he wasn't adverse to killing, either. But he was also a great politician and he realized that he could unite Japan faster through bribery, alliances, and political maneuvering rather than constant war, which is exactly what he did. Instead of fighting Ieyasu, for instance, he made him his ally.

"Because Hideyoshi was a commoner and not a noble, he couldn't take the title of Shōgun. Although he couldn't get all the titles he craved, Hideyoshi was still able to amass considerable power and wealth. At one point he had a tearoom made of solid gold, and he was famous for the opulence of his court and castles. When he died in 1598, he left a young son as his heir, with Japan governed by a council of five regents. This led to a dangerous and unstable political situation.

"Ieyasu Tokugawa was one of the five regents. He had been waiting for years for his chance to rule Japan and he eventually became the chief opponent of the Toyotomi clan. Through threats and victory in battle, he gradually eroded the Toyotomi's power. It took him almost fifteen years to eventually destroy the Toyotomis. During this unstable period the legend of the Toyotomi blades was born.

"According to the legend, in 1614 the Toyotomis hid a portion of their treasure as a hedge against future battles with Ieyasu. They wanted a financial reserve because their battle with Ieyasu was a protracted one. A message revealing the hiding place for the treasure was cut on the blades of six swords by the swordsmith Kannemori. Each sword had a piece of the message, and all six swords would be needed to find the treasure. The swords were given to six trusted retainers of the Toyotomi clan. Each retainer given a blade did not know the exact identity of the other five, only that there were six blades in all. Only Hideyoshi's widow and his son knew which six families had a blade. That way, no one would be tempted to change sides, taking the treasure with them.

"Unfortunately for the Toyotomis, Ieyasu managed to destroy Osaka castle, the stronghold of the Toyotomis, and take over the country before the Toyotomis could muster the strength to defeat him. Hideyoshi's widow and son perished with the fall of Osaka castle, and apparently the Toyotomis were never able to use their secret hoard of treasure."

"How do you know this?"

Sonoda-san smiled. "My family was one of the ones entrusted with a blade. In fact, the Kannemori sword I own today has been passed down in my family for almost four hundred years. My father told me this legend, as his father told it and his father before him. The original recipient of the blade got it directly from the hands of Yodo Domo, Hideyoshi's widow. He was told about the six blades, and that it was necessary for all six blades to be put next to each other or the treasure could not be found. He then was told to guard the blade until it was called for. We've been doing that ever since, and I strongly believe in the legend."

"Do you know how the blades reveal where the treasure is?"

"My family was never told that, but I think it's some kind of message. When you get all six blades together you can decipher a message that tells you the hiding place."

"Could the blades form something besides a message?"

"Such as?"

"A map."

Sonoda rubbed his chin. "I've always assumed that the pictures formed words, but I suppose they could be a map. I've never thought of it that way."

"Where are the blades now?" Mariko asked.

"Over the centuries, I'm sure the blades were passed down from generation to generation, but since I don't know the five other families who received a blade, it's impossible to know where they are now. I'm sure not all families were as lucky as mine in their ability to retain the blades. I know one blade ended up in the Japan National Museum, but it was stolen just this year. Hirota-san tells me that you own one that you bought in the United States. I'd love to see it. My guess is that it was taken from Japan at the end of World War II as a souvenir. A great many swords left Japan during that period."

"I think I know about two others," I said.

Sonoda's eyebrows shot up. "Really?"

"I think so. One was sold at a New York auction and was used as a decoration in a rich man's apartment. A few weeks ago it was stolen and the owner was killed. The police think the man was a member of the Mafia and that he was killed by organized crime, but the sword was stolen as part of the murder. I'm beginning to think it might be the real reason for the murder. The second sword was in the Dutch Shipping Museum in Rotterdam. It also was stolen, just a couple of days after the murder in New York. Both swords were made by Kannemori and both swords had patterns incised on the blade. Look." I took the faxes from my pocket and showed them to him.

Sonoda-san took the faxes from me eagerly, his hand positively shaking with excitement. He peered at the faxes. "Great!" he said.

"Are these blades new to you?" I asked.

"Yes. There's no central registry of swords around the world, and unless one is auctioned through a recognized source like Sotheby's, which distributes an international catalog of Japanese swords and other Japanese works of art auctioned in New York and London, it's almost impossible to know if a sword goes on the market."

"Couldn't you know that by computer?" Mariko asked.

Sonoda-san grinned. "I don't own a computer. Even a VCR is baffling to me."

"I don't think it would help much if you did," I said. "Most art auctions are not currently computerized, and despite what people think, most knowledge is not on the Internet. There's just too much knowledge still on paper, and no money to computerize it or even index it. For instance, I'd be surprised if the Dutch Shipping Museum even has an Internet site, much less an on-line catalog of its collection. I learned about the swords because they were stolen and mentioned in news stories."

"I thought these blades were lost forever," Mr. Sonoda ruminated. "Yours, mine, and the three blades stolen in New York, Rotterdam, and Tokyo. That's five blades. Do you know where the sixth blade is?"

"No. But I think whoever's stealing the blades must know where it is. After all, what good is five-sixths of a map?"

"But why would anyone steal the blades now?"

"I was hoping maybe you could tell me that. Are these blades especially famous or symbolic of Japan?"

"No. The legend of the Toyotomi blades is an obscure one. Why is that important?"

"Because I've been told that the Yakuza is especially conservative so I thought they might want the blades for their symbolic value."

"Do you think the Yakuza is involved in this?"

"I don't know. I'm still confused about exactly who is involved in this and why. Do you think the legend of the blades is true?"

"You mean that the blades point to a treasure?"

"That's right."

Sonoda sighed. "My family has believed that for four hundred years, and I believe it, too. But I'm a romantic, and I want to believe in something that is so much a part of my family heritage. The patterns on the blades are unique and each blade is different. They could fit together somehow, but how would you know what order to put them in?"

"Your blade has a number on the tang, right?"

"Yes it does. In addition to the usual markings with the year it was made, it has the number three."

"My blade might have a number on it, too. When I get back to Tokyo, Professor Hirota will have a rubbing of it for me and I'll be able to see. If it does, I'll bet the numbers indicate the order that the blades should be placed."

"Interesting," Sonoda said. He picked up the faxes and looked at them. "It's too bad these faxes are of such poor quality. But you'd also need to get rubbings or pictures of all the blades with their handles removed. Then you could see if they all had a number. It would be nice to put the blades next to each other and then maybe we could see if they really formed a message or a map."

"I've been thinking about that, too. I work as a computer programmer and I think these images can be computer enhanced so we can see the patterns,"

"Really?" He studied the faxes closely. "That's amazing, but one of these blades has the handle attached. Even if you could see the patterns on the blades, you wouldn't know the proper order for the blades. Plus, you're still missing one of the blades, which would make it impossible to decipher a message or complete a map."

Mariko patted me on the arm. "He'll figure out a way around that."

"You have more faith in me than I have," I told her. "Right now I don't have a clue about how I'll solve the problem of the missing blade or the inability to see the numbers on the tang of some of the blades. I'm like a man groping his way down a dark road with a dim flashlight. I'm interested in seeing just far enough ahead not to stumble. I can't see the end of the road."

"But if you can keep moving forward you will come to the end of the road, even if you can't see the end point. Isn't that true?" Mariko smiled.

"I guess you're right," I said. "But that assumes that I don't come to the edge of a cliff or anything. Then I can't go forward without falling off and killing myself."

"It interests me that you want to solve mysteries," Sonoda-san said.

"Why?"

"Righting things that are wrong seems to be an American ideal, but I get the feeling that maybe your Japanese heritage has something to do with your desire to get mysteries solved."

"What to you mean?"

"It's a Confucian ideal to have things in balance and working in harmony. Like it or not, a lot of Japanese culture springs from this Confucian view of the world. That's different than the typical Western thirst for justice. Something like Victor Hugo's *Les Misérables,* where Javert pursues Jean Valjean to satisfy some technicality of the law, is very peculiar to us.

"In our view of the world, individual justice can exist only after the larger society is in harmony. In fact we're supposed to sacrifice our individual desires for the good of the family, the company, or the country. I'm curious about what motivates you to get involved in these mysteries."

"I don't know. I just get a feeling that something is wrong and I want to put it right. Until recently I acted like your description of the Confucian ideal. I subordinated my personal desires and took a safe path, a path with as little conflict as possible. I know that choice came from my mother, who always advised me not to make waves. Lately, I've found that it can be exciting to make waves. When I met Mariko it came as a shock to me that she was starting over in life, giving up a good job with a bank and trying to make a new career as an actress. I thought she was crazy." That drew a smile from her. "But playing it safe didn't work out for me. The company I worked for downsized me out of a job, and the work and sacrifices I made for that job seem pretty silly. Now I think I was crazy to play it safe. I know I'm influenced by my Japanese heritage, but I think I'm ready to take risks. I don't know if that risk taking is Japanese or American, but it's what I want now."

17

On the return train trip to Tokyo, I had a lot to think about. My growing curiosity about the blades was now inflamed by Sonoda-san's talk of treasure, and I mused about the possibility of solving the mystery. I had access to images of five of the six blades, but it wasn't clear sailing.

First, one blade was still missing, and I didn't have too many ideas about how I could find it. Next the clarity of the faxes of the Rotterdam and New York blades would present a challenge in seeing what was on those blades. The meaning of the long line on my blade still puzzled me. All the other patterns were pretty clear, in terms of identifying forest and temples and mountains, but the wandering line was a puzzle. Finally, I was still scared about the Yakuza catching me before I could leave Japan. Oh, and I had miscounted the number of socks to pack and I realized I was going to run out of clean socks before it was time to return home.

That last problem, at least, had solutions. I could fly home in dirty socks or have the hotel wash a couple of pair for me. The rest of the problems, however, stumped me, worried me, or just plain made me nervous.

During these musings I stared absently out the train window, trying to come up with some answers. Mariko sat next to me, and sensing my mood, silently read a book on kabuki in preparation for seeing a play in Tokyo's Kabukiza Theater. As we sat together in silence it occurred to me that a good friend is someone you can stay with for hours without the compulsion to fill the voids with conversation. Mariko was more than a lover, she was a good friend, and in this life it's often easier to find a lover than a true friend.

When we got back to Tokyo I sent a couple of pairs of socks down to the hotel laundry. One problem solved. Then I took out the faxes Junko had given me and studied them for several minutes. Although I've never done it myself, I thought the faxes might be candidates for computer enhancement. Of course, in Japan I didn't even have a laptop computer, but I figured that when I returned to Los Angeles I might be able to hunt up someone who had the software and equipment to help me. If that didn't look good, maybe I could get better copies of the originals by writing New York and Rotterdam.

The show sent a car for me three hours before airtime. Mariko was going to do some shopping and join me later at the studio, so I stopped at the hotel concierge and had him write down the studio name and address in Japanese for her. I didn't want her ending up at some weird place like the guy in the match story.

When I got to the studio the first order of business was to sit down with Junko and tell her what I had learned about the blades from Sonoda-san. "Did Professor Hirota return my blade?" I asked when I finished.

"Just as he promised."

"Did he also give us a rubbing of the blade?"

"He did."

"Is there a number on the tang of my blade?"

"Yes there is. A six."

"I knew it!"

"What are you excited about?"

I told her my theories about the blades forming a map. She seemed very interested, especially when I talked about the possibility of unraveling the mystery.

"Do you think that's possible?" she asked.

"I don't know. I've been thinking about it ever since I got back from Kyoto and if the mystery can't be solved completely, at least we can uncover a good deal more information about it in a rather short period of time."

"How can that be true? The mystery is over four hundred years old. Why do you think more information can be developed now?"

"I think somebody else has done just that, that's why the swords are being stolen. I can't believe it's a coincidence that these swords are being stolen within a relatively short period of time. One of the swords is missing, but I've also got my sword. If somebody is stealing the blades, they haven't got mine yet. They're probably also missing at least one other blade.

"If they've got the New York and Rotterdam blades, though, they do have a big advantage. The fax quality will make it difficult to bring out the patterns on the blades. I was thinking of contacting Rotterdam and New York to see if I could get them to mail me clearer copies, but that still might not help. I think the pictures have to be made a lot bigger and a lot clearer."

"What are you talking about?"

"These fax pictures would be good candidates for computer enhancing to bring out the detail in the patterns on the blades. I haven't done it myself, but I'm generally familiar with how computer enhancing works, and I think it can be done. Do you do that kind of work here at the station?"

"No, we don't, but one of our sponsors is Nissan, and they have a research project going that uses that sort of technique. We've done a couple of pieces on it. The pieces were a combination of puff piece and genuine news story, but they were both well received. Nissan is developing a navigational system for cars, so they are putting together a digitized map of Japan from computerized satellite photographs. They've developed all sorts of software to analyze and enhance the photos and ways to turn pictures into digital images. It's all high-tech stuff and Japanese tend to love high technology."

"You also tend to love tradition. It's a strange combination."

"It is, but Japanese culture is full of strange combinations. That's one thing that always seems to fascinate visitors."

"I think it's possible that high technology could be applied to this old mystery. I don't have the resources myself, but maybe I could interest someone when I get back to Los Angeles."

"How long do you think it would take to solve the mystery?"

"I didn't say I could solve the mystery. I just said I could come up with a lot more information about it. There are often mysteries that can't be solved. This might turn out to be one of them."

"Would you mind if they asked you some questions about all this on tonight's show?"

"No, I wouldn't."

"Great. What I'd like you to do now is review the lead-in clip. This is what we'll show before the live interview with you. It runs about three minutes." Junko popped a tape into a machine. I sat there watching the piece she'd put together to introduce my segment of the show as she translated the narrative. She had done a nice job combining stock footage of L.A. with newsreel clips to explain the murder case I'd solved.

When the tape was over she asked me, "Well, what do you think?"

"I think you did a great job. That'll be a good introduction to the interview."

"Are you nervous about the interview?"

"A little bit. I've never been on TV before, much less live TV."

"Would you like some hints?" Junko asked.

"I'd love some hints."

"Well, before the show you'll be taken to makeup. A lot of people feel foolish having makeup put on them, but just relax and let the technicians do their job."

"What happens after I'm beautiful?"

She smiled. "Then you'll wait for your interview. It might seem forever, but the interviews are only a few minutes long, and Nagahara-san and Yukiko-chan will actually fill up a lot of that time just chatting between themselves and reacting to things you say. I'll be translating from Japanese to English and you'll have an earpiece so you can hear me. Buzz Sugimoto will translate your answers from English to Japanese.

"Sugimoto-san is doing the translation from English to Japanese so that viewers will hear a man's voice when you speak. I'm actually a much better translator," she said proudly, "but viewers sometimes find it jarring when they hear a woman's voice when a man is speaking.

"When you get on the set, sit on the edge of your chair and

lean forward slightly. That comes across on camera like you're alert and full of energy. Also turn your body about fifteen degrees so your head is at a slight angle to your shoulders. That also looks much better on camera. Smile and relax and just try to be natural. Television is a very intimate medium, and if you just talk to Nagahara-san and Yukiko-chan the way you talk to me, you'll come across great.

"On *News Pop* we don't practice any of the *Sixty Minutes*–style journalism and we won't ask you embarrassing questions. Nagahara-san and Yukiko-chan have some scripted questions that they use to kick off the interview. I'll give you a copy of those in English so you can formulate some answers, but try to answer them as naturally as possible on camera. Don't work out a speech or anything.

"Nagahara-san will take the lead after the first few questions. I know he looks like an old fuddy-duddy, but he's actually an excellent journalist. He started his career right after the Korean War and did a lot of coverage of the Vietnam War for Japanese television. He's an old pro and if you get in any sort of trouble he'll be able to step in and carry you until the end of the interview. I know you'll do a great job on tonight's show. There was quite a bit of interest in Japan about the case you were involved in and this new material you've given me on the Toyotomi blades is also very interesting. Remember, just talk to them like you talk to me and the results will be fantastic."

With that pep talk Junko left me to watch TV or read until it was time to go into makeup. They took me to makeup, and even though I did feel foolish wearing it, I took Junko's advice and tried to relax. After makeup they put me in the greenroom (which in this case was light blue) where you wait to appear on the TV show. There were only two segments on the show, and I was to be the last segment. Mariko was waiting for me in the greenroom, and I stopped her before she could give me a kiss of greeting.

"You'll mess up my makeup," I told her.

"You haven't even been on TV yet and you're already turning into a temperamental star."

Junko had told me that the first segment was on a housewife from Osaka who had organized a group of other housewives to stop fraud from door-to-door vendors. She, her daughter, and her husband were also in the greenroom with me. They were all polite when I came in, but since they didn't speak any English and we didn't speak any Japanese, we really couldn't have any conversation.

It seemed like the time just crawled until the *News Pop* show started. Right before the start of the show, the housewife was taken from the greenroom to the set. Her husband and daughter waved good-bye to her like she was being taken off to be shipped to a penal colony on Mars.

The opening credits of *News Pop* are computer graphics that take a fireworks display and swirl the exploding bursts until they form a couple of kanji that I assume mean *News Pop*. The kanji dissolve and reform over a map of the world. The segment on the Osaka housewife started with a video clip just as mine would and then they cut to the live interview.

I can't say I understood what the story of the Osaka housewife was all about. Mariko was as baffled as me. It had something to do with very aggressive street vendors who apparently sell Japanese *futons,* or quilts, door-to-door. It showed a clip of some kind of scientific lab taking a futon apart and measuring it and its contents, so I guess maybe people were being swindled and not getting the quality of quilt they thought they were buying.

The housewife was not very lively during the interview. She sat at the desk with her hands folded demurely in her lap answering the questions with a *hai,* or yes, and occasionally giggling and putting her hands up to her mouth when Nagahara-san or Yukiko-chan cracked some kind of joke. It didn't seem like much of a performance to me, but her husband and child seemed delighted. They were understandably glued to the television set in the greenroom, laughing when a joke was made and even clapping their hands together in a sort of applause to her hai's, as if they were the most eloquent statements in the world.

It's great to have support and I appreciated Mariko being there. With the simultaneous translation, however, Mariko wouldn't understand my interview. I'd be opening my mouth but Sugimoto's voice speaking Japanese would be what was broadcast.

I was pretty nervous when it was my time to go on the show. An aide came to get me out of the greenroom, and Mariko blew me a kiss. The show was in the midst of a commercial and Nagahara-san and Yukiko-chan both bowed politely as I sat down in my seat. I sort of dipped my head. The whole question of bowing is a really involved one, with all sorts of rules about how far you bow, who bows first, and what all the different kinds of bows mean. I realized that the three of us sitting at the desk looked Japanese, but with me the Japanese veneer was literally only skin deep and there were all sorts of things I didn't know.

The sword I'd brought with me was put on the counter in front of me as a prop. I took a look at it and it looked great. The handle had been rewrapped with glossy black silk cords.

Technicians hooked me up with a mike to my lapel and fitted an earpiece to my left ear, which would be away from the camera. As soon as the piece was in my ear I heard Junko's voice.

"Are you nervous? Just nod 'cause they're not ready to do a sound check on your mike yet."

I nodded the affirmative.

"Well you look good," she said in my earpiece. "You shouldn't be too nervous. You know what questions they're going to start with, but I want you to know that I did talk to Nagahara-san about all the information you've dug up on the Toyotomi blades and he's very interested in it. It's likely that he'll ask you some questions about it. He's an old-time newshound, and if he senses a story he's always interested in pursuing it."

There was a pause, and Junko said, "Why don't you say something to me so we can get a sound check."

"Do you think he'll ask many questions about the Toyotomi blades?"

"I don't know. We're doing live interviews and one of the exciting things about live interviews is you can't predict what will happen. Why don't you say something else because we want to double check the sound levels."

"Okay. Testing one, two, three. Testing."

"Not very original."

"Now is the winter of our discontent made glorious summer by this sun of York."

"Still not original, but certainly classy."

Yukiko-chan, who evidently spoke some English, looked at me a little surprised and said, "Shakespeare."

I laughed and nodded. She laughed too. It was just what I needed to put me at ease. On one of the monitors, set in front of the desk, I could see that the piece about the murder was coming to a conclusion. I started to settle down, but then remembering what Junko told me, I slid to the edge of my seat, turned my body slightly, and tried to look bright and charming.

Nagahara-sun started speaking and Junko starting translating simultaneously in English. It was sort of a weird experience and I learned that I could follow things much better if I tried to ignore what Nagahara-san was saying and just listened to the translation in my ear.

We went through the prepared questions rather quickly and I tried to give what I thought were complete and interesting responses. It's hard to know how successful I was, but I was determined that I wasn't going to just sit there and say "yes" like the housewife.

It seemed like I had been answering questions forever, but during a short pause when Nagahara-san was talking to Yukiko-chan, Junko said, "We still have several minutes to fill. Nagahara-san is telling Yukiko-chan a little bit about the Toyotomi blades mystery you're now involved in."

Nagahara-san turned back to me and, through Junko's translation, said, "I understand that you've been working on another mystery in the time you've been in Japan."

"Yes I have. It's kind of a strange mystery that's tied into Japanese history." I launched into the story of the Toyotomi blades, adding what Junko had found out about the robberies and murder in New York as well as the robberies in Rotterdam and in Tokyo.

I picked up the sword in front of me and slid it from its scabbard, showing Nagahara-san and Yukiko-chan the pattern on the blades. Throughout my dissertation, Nagahara-san and Yukiko-chan had been making encouraging comments, such as "Is that so," "How interesting," and "Really." This is a speech pattern in Japanese that they often use on the telephone to encourage the speaker. Even though I knew this was just a polite convention, I actually found it comforting that they were murmuring these encouragements.

When I finished recounting what I knew about the history of the blades as well as the current goings on, Nagahara-san said, "You found all this out in less than a week here in Tokyo?"

"Yes. I got help from Sonoda-san in Kyoto as well as the *News Pop* research staff. When I get back to Los Angeles, I intend to work on the mystery a bit more because I find it a fascinating one."

"I think it is extremely interesting, too," Nagahara-san said. "But wouldn't it be easier to work on the mystery in Tokyo instead of Los Angeles?"

"Yes it would, but unfortunately I'm scheduled to return to Los Angeles tomorrow."

"If *News Pop* paid your expenses and perhaps got you some additional research help, could you stay in Tokyo another week and spend some more time investigating the mystery of the Toyotomi blades?" Nagahara-san said to me.

That took me by surprise, but I figured what the hell, I was unemployed and had no pressing engagements in Los Angeles. My girlfriend was here in Tokyo, anyway, and I'd gotten used to maid service, laundry service, limos, and restaurant-cooked meals paid for by someone else during my stay in Tokyo.

"I think I can stay," I said. "And with the help of the *News Pop* staff I also think that we can unravel a bit more of this particular mystery. I can't promise to solve it in a week, but I'm sure that with a little bit more time we can uncover more information about the Toyotomi blades and the treasure that they're supposed to be the key to."

"All right then," Nagahara-san said. "Please consider that we've given you an invitation to stay another week in Tokyo at our expense, and please come back on the show next week and tell about how much progress you've made."

"That's a generous offer," I stammered. "I'll certainly do my best."

O kay, I've got a big mouth. Sometimes it starts working before my brain is in gear. As soon as the closing credits for *News Pop* started crawling across the monitor screens in the studio, I knew I just had a major meltdown. I had an image of gears popping out of my ears as I tried to figure out why I had taken on this challenge.

If you're raised with an Asian background, the consequences of a big mouth can be dire because of the problem of face. Face is the notion that your life is tightly entwined with your family, your ancestors, your clan, your village, your company, and your country. When some disgrace or insult falls on you, it also falls on all the entities to which you're connected. The shame is magnified a thousandfold. Face is often used to excuse all sorts of ridiculous behavior in books and movies. Unfortunately, it's also a motivator for some equally ridiculous real-life actions.

A few years ago the captain of a cargo vessel had the misfortune to get caught in a severe mid-Pacific storm. The captain might have avoided the worst of the storm by taking a longer route, but he was anxious to reach his destination. His ship was stuffed with Mazda automobiles and during the storm some of the cars broke free from their tie-downs and caused considerable damage. Almost one hundred cars were damaged.

Other captains might have been able to shrug off the incident. The marine insurance would pay for the damage and no people were injured. But this captain was Japanese, and he had lost face. So when the vessel finally came into port he went to the deck where the worse damage occurred and tried to commit *seppuku*, which is a ritual suicide vulgarly known as *hara kiri* (slit the belly). Unfortunately for the captain, his archaic gesture turned from tragedy to farce because of one little detail: He didn't bring a big enough knife. In the old days they committed seppuku with a short sword. The captain brought a pocketknife.

He stabbed himself over twenty times. Stabbing yourself in the abdomen can be a painful and slow death, so seppuku usually involved an assistant who would cut off the head of the person committing the suicide. The captain had no assistant, and despite the number of stab wounds he had inflicted on himself, the crew was able to find him and get him to a hospital before he bled to death. Instead of dying to apologize for his lack of ability, the captain confirmed this lack in his botched suicide.

I didn't have a penknife, but my mouth was able to inflict all the damage necessary. I was supposed to uncover more information about the Toyotomi blades by staying in Japan another week. The truth was that for all I knew I could stay in Japan another year and still not find out any more information. When I thought of it, most of what I had now was given to me by Sonoda-san or Junko. My major contribution was figuring out that the blades might fit together to form a map, and I wasn't even sure if that was accurate.

By agreeing to the challenge I ran the risk of embarrassing myself in a culture where embarrassment can be acute and serious. Of course, it wasn't as if all my friends and neighbors would know what I had done. But I would know. The Japanese part of my Japanese-American heritage would be mortified by the loss of face if I didn't come through with something.

Junko and Sugimoto joined us in the studio. Yukiko-chan and Nagahara-san seemed very excited after the show. Sugimoto looked glum, as if Nagahara-san's interest in the story was somehow a personal slight against him. Forming the Yin to Sugimoto's Yang, Junko was simply beaming and basking in what I took to be praise from Nagahara-san and Yukiko-chan.

When I asked Junko what they were telling her, she just smiled and said, "They're very enthused about this story. We're going to give it a big buildup over the next week. We got a pretty good response from the Sansei detective angle we played this week in our promos and next week should be even better because every school kid knows about Hideyoshi Toyotomi. This would be just like an American audience finding out about a treasure hidden by George Washington or Abraham Lincoln."

"But I'm not sure that I can find the treasure," I protested. "I just said that I'd try to get more information about the blades by next week's show."

"Oh, we know that," Junko said airily. "Nagahara-san doesn't expect you to solve the mystery. He just wants you to do your best over the next week. Whatever you come up with we'll put into the most positive light possible. The big pull for next week's show will be to find out what you came up with. You had a highly rated show in the States about Al Capone's vault. When they opened it on live television they found a bunch of dirt and a few old bottles. The sponsors got their audience, though, which was the real point of the show."

"But I'm going to need some help to work on this. I don't want to end up looking stupid on next week's show."

"I called one of the executives at Nissan. The staff hunted down his home phone number for me. We discussed your need for help with computer enhancement and he agreed to get Nissan to help you."

"But wouldn't it be easier to get originals sent from Rotterdam or New York?"

"Sure, but that would cut into several minutes of video tape showing Nissan's technological prowess. They're one of our main sponsors and that kind of piece won't hurt them and it certainly won't hurt the show."

"But what if I don't find out anything new about the blades in the next week?"

"Oh, I'm sure you will." Junko looked almost effervescent. She had an expression on her face that said the possibility that I wouldn't find anything more about the blades was unthinkable. Unfortunately, that was all I could think of.

When I got back to the greenroom, Mariko gave me a big kiss.

"We don't have to worry about your makeup now! You looked great, but I didn't understand what was going on. You opened your mouth and all this Japanese came out. I started giggling. It looked like one of those badly dubbed kung fu movies. The two anchors seemed extremely pleased at the end."

"They should be pleased. I told them I'd stay another week in Tokyo and solve the mystery of the Toyotomi blades for them."

"You what?"

"Well, actually I said I'd work on the mystery and see what I could come up with. But it's obvious that they've got pretty high expectations."

"Ken, why would you say you'd solve the mystery?"

"I didn't say I could solve the mystery. I said I would work on the mystery. I don't know if the mystery can be solved. It will let me stay another week with you here in Tokyo."

"But what about the Yakuza who are after you?"

"I'd forgotten that little detail," I said. "Thanks for reminding me."

The world headquarters for Nissan Motors occupies two imposing towers on the outskirts of the Ginza district. It was walking distance from the Imperial Hotel, but I took a cab. The talk of the Yakuza the previous night did not go unheeded.

In a small courtyard outside the front entrance of the building were a series of ancient building blocks projecting from the stone floor of the courtyard like weathered dragon's teeth. They looked centuries old and appeared to be pieces from some ancient castle. Just a few feet away was the lobby and showroom for Nissan, with new cars basking under lighting that made them look positively glossy. The dichotomy of old and new is the prevailing theme in Japan.

A crew from *News Pop* was there to film me walking into the Nissan building. They made me do it three times so they could get different angles of me walking into the building with the single camera they brought. It made me feel silly, especially as a small crowd gathered, and I was grateful when the camera crew left so I could go about the business of trying to enhance the fax images.

In the lobby I was greeted by a pleasant young woman sitting at a reception desk. Her English was weak, but good enough to understand that I was there for a meeting with a Mr. Kiyohara. I cooled my heels for a few minutes looking at the new cars and another young woman appeared to take me to an elevator. Once we were on the working floors of the building, the shiny newness of the lobby was left behind and the halls and decor became very austere. The office she took me to was very much like the others I had seen in Japan, with rows of tiny desks facing each other, all jammed together. The desks were cluttered with papers, little souvenirs, photos, and people. Although several employees looked up as I entered, most seemed hard at work.

At the end of each row was a slightly larger desk positioned so that the person sitting at it could look down the rows. Here the supervisor or manager sat. It gave the office a crowded but intimate atmosphere and allowed management to know almost through osmosis who was diligent and working hard and who wasn't.

Mr. Kiyohara was a tall, thin man with a soft-spoken manner. He was quite handsome, with sharp cheekbones and a square-cut chin. His eyes sparkled with intelligence. His English had a mumbled quality to it, as if he wasn't quite confident of his command of the language and didn't want to speak out, but I found it very understandable.

"The television program explained what you're trying to do. I hope we can help," Kiyohara said after we had introduced ourselves. He seemed to be in his mid-forties and his face had a serious demeanor that I've noticed on other adult Japanese, but with Kiyohara I got the impression that the seriousness was a mask and underneath there was a lively sense of humor to match the intelligence shown in the eyes.

Kiyohara led me to a conference room. Like the rest of the office, it was positively spartan, with a gray metal table with chairs of green vinyl and metal. He introduced me to several younger Japanese whom he identified as team members who worked in the area of photo enhancement, and I noted that two of the team members were women.

"Ohara-san has explained to me that you're interested in enhancing the image on a photograph," Kiyohara began when we had all settled down around the table. "As you might know, Nissan not only makes automobiles, but we also get ourselves involved with a lot of other things. We make boats, looms for weaving, and even guided missiles. A Nissan rocket put the first Japanese space satellite in orbit, as a matter of fact.

"Because of our involvement with satellites, we've been working on image enhancing to improve the quality of weather photographs. One of the projects is a complete digital map of Japan that we want to use in a navigation system for cars. In addition to roads, the map will show all of Japan's major features and many of its more significant buildings.

"To do this, we had to develop techniques that would allow computers to analyze photographs, pick up features, and resolve them into some kind of mathematical pattern. The United States is the leader in this area, but I think we still have the facilities to help you."

I took the faxes out of my pocket and placed them on the table. "It would help enormously if we could get enhanced images of these. If you saw last night's show, it should be clear how helpful it would be to see the patterns on the blades." I pushed the faxes over to Kiyohara.

He picked them up and looked at them with interest. Other members of the team craned their necks to take a peak.

"You'll notice the sword blade is clearly visible," I said. "But because of the size of the photo and the quality of the fax, I can't make out the symbols on the blade. Even if I get originals, I'm not sure about how the quality of the image will be maintained if we try to enlarge the photos to a size that's useful for comparison with other images of blades I have." I took the copies of the three blade rubbings I now had and gave them to Kiyohara. As promised, Hirota had given me a rubbing of my own blade, and I had Junko make a photocopy of this rubbing, too.

"Ideally, I'd like an image that was the same size as these photocopies of rubbings. I think the blades fit together to form a map, and I'd like to be able to manipulate the rubbings and images to see if I can fit them together."

"How will you know what it's a map of?" Kiyohara said. "Is there some reference point so you know what you'll be looking at?"

I sighed. "No, and I'm actually missing a piece of the map because I don't have a rubbing or picture of one of the blades. I think there are six of them, but as you can see I only have five represented with what I have. In fact, I don't even know in what order they fit together, but I figure that I'll just approach things one step at a time. With only a week until the next show I have to keep moving, even if I'm not always making progress."

"Well, we can help you with movement and hopefully it will also be progress. Are you familiar with the technique of photo enhancing?"

"I know a little bit about it, but if you have the time I wouldn't mind having an explanation about what you are going to do with the faxes."

"Well, in concept it's really quite simple, although it's part art as well as part science. It does take a lot of programming and computer power to accomplish it on a large scale, but we have big computers at our data center to do all sorts of design and engineering tasks; photo enhancement is just one of them.

"What we do is divide the photograph, such as the photographs on these two faxes, into a series of tiny squares. With photographs of this size, the squares will be about one-tenth the diameter of a hair: very, very small. Then we take the section of the photograph that we are interested in and digitize it. That is, we give a number to the square, based on its color value.

"In a good black-and-white photograph you should have all sorts of tones, ranging from almost a pure white to a pure black. You can measure these tones and apply a number to each tone, let's say from one to ten. One is white and ten is black. The gray values in the middle would have numbers like two, four, or six. This way we can number, or digitize, each spot on the photograph.

"The actual numbers we use are much more complex. They go up to 1,024 for the shade and over sixteen thousand for the hue, or color. Still, the process is the same as the one-through-ten example I gave you. By scanning the photograph and taking a reading at each of the tiny squares that we have marked out on the photograph, we can apply a value to how light or dark that square is.

"After we have digitized the photograph, we can keep the values for each point on the photo in computer memory and save them for later manipulation. Let's say that on one small portion of the photograph we end up with a pattern like this."

Kiyohara took out a pencil and drew a diagram on a pad of paper.

```
777777777
777577777
333333333
333333333
```

"Remember, this pattern represents a very small section of the photograph, perhaps the size of the head of a pin. You'll see that we have a row of darker colors here, represented by sevens, right next to a row of lighter colors, represented by threes. We have computer programs that look through the patterns and find situations such as this. Our assumption here is we are looking at the edge of something, a straight edge against a lighter background. Based on that assumption, we would adjust the one dot which is out of place, here."

He put his pencil down on the 5 that broke up the string of 7s.

"Our working assumption is that this five is a flaw, a problem with the photograph and that what is really represented here is a straight line, so that all these values should be seven. Therefore, we would darken this single dot to a seven. We would go through the entire photograph looking for these types of flaws and make the dots lighter or darker, depending on what the surrounding values look like."

Kiyohara smiled. "That is the science portion of it. Now the art comes in. We have someone sit in front of a screen and look at these patterns. He can look at the entire photograph or he can zoom a section up, to look at the individual dots that make up a section. Using a light pen and a keyboard, he can lighten or darken dots to enhance a particular section of the photograph. The computer programs do surprisingly well in enhancing the photographs on their own, but sometimes you also need a human eye to look at the patterns to see if they make sense. Some things, such as vegetation, don't have regular, sharp-edged forms, and it's hard to program the computer to do a completely accurate job."

He placed his finger on one of the faxes. "This, however, is a steel sword. Fine geometric shapes, hard edges. It should come through photo enhancement very nicely."

"How long will this take?" I asked.

"I don't think it will take too long. Perhaps one hour, perhaps two hours. Would you like to wait or would you like to come back?"

"If you don't mind, I'd like to wait. I'm quite anxious to see what the results are."

I spent a pleasant hour sipping green tea and looking at car brochures until Kiyohara returned. He handed over an enhanced photograph of one of my faxes and said, "Is it good enough for your purposes?"

I looked at the enhanced photograph and smiled. "Perfect."

20

By the end of the morning I had two enhanced prints of the blades from Rotterdam and New York. A Nissan stockholder might think the computer power burned up to get me those prints might be better spent designing cup holders for minivans, but I was pretty pleased with the results. On the Rotterdam blade I could make out a single slash on the tang that Kiyohara told me was the number one, and on both blades I could see the patterns. One had what looked like a village on it and the other had a mountain and a waterfall. Just as important, I got an offer of more help.

"We've been talking about this mystery," he told me when he gave me the finished prints, "and perhaps there's more we can do for you. The digitized map of Japan we've been working on has things like temples and mountains on it, just like the designs that are on these blades. If you're right about the blades forming a map, maybe we can match that map against our digitized map of Japan to help you pinpoint where the treasure is."

"Can you help me figure out where the blade I'm missing is? There are supposed to be six blades, and I've only got images for five."

He laughed. "No. Perhaps you should go to a . . ." He sought the English word. "A psychic." I wasn't sure he was kidding.

I spent the rest of the day working on finding the sixth blade with very little to show for it. Junko called Professor Hirota, but his assistant said he was already off on another trip. I talked to Sonoda-san in Kyoto, but although he seemed pleased to talk to me, he wasn't able to give me any more information than he had when I was in Kyoto. Junko and I searched every database to which *News Pop* had access, in English and Japanese, and we even tried calling the U.S. to try some databases I knew about. No luck.

Mariko and I had dinner together, and she told me about her sightseeing that day. I was so engrossed in trying to figure out a way to find the sixth blade that I wasn't much company. While Mariko watched an English-language movie on TV, I sat on the bed looking at the enhanced prints and the rubbings of the blades, trying to make sense of them. When we fell asleep I dreamed about colored sword blades dancing in the air, forming endless patterns as they combined in different combinations. If Walt Disney had been Japanese, perhaps something like that would have been in *Fantasia*.

The next morning the light woke me. I had forgotten to close the curtains in the room. I looked at the clock and saw it was only 6:10 A.M. I was tired, but not sleepy, and after lying in bed a couple of minutes, I slipped out of bed and got up.

Without waking the still sleeping Mariko, I dressed quickly, putting on a jogging suit and my running shoes. I got my jacket from the closet, wrote a quick note to Mariko, and checked to make sure I had my passport and wallet.

I walked out the front door of the Imperial and strolled to the corner where a light would let me cross the street to Hibiya Park. The chill air invigorated me and I started some simple stretching exercises while waiting for the light to change. When the light turned green I started jogging across the street and into the park.

Despite being bordered by busy streets, the park was quiet in the early morning hours, although by no means lifeless. As I jogged along I came across a group of Japanese students standing in their black uniforms doing calisthenics. Another student, acting as exercise leader, stood in front of the group of eight or ten of them.

I went past a lake with a fountain decorated with bronze cranes. The graceful bronze birds curved into the morning air.

The earth by the side of the path was slightly muddy. It was fall and the bite of winter was in the air. Coming from California where there really isn't a winter, I felt both wonder and excitement at the ancient cycle of seasons surrounding me.

As I curved around the lake, I saw a pavilion over to the side. In the pavilion a middle-aged man sat reading. I wondered idly what he was reading and why he decided to get up so early in the morning to read it in the chilled park.

I continued jogging and came across another path. I cut to the right on the path and slowed down to a walk. I felt better. My brain was clearer. With the short jog and the morning air, I started to relax, looking about me at the trees and the foliage.

Up ahead I saw a small snack stand and decided I would stop and try to get some hot chocolate or coffee. I walked up to the stand and an old man in an olive jacket, fatigue pants, and rubber boots was standing behind the counter. He grinned a toothy grin at me and gave some greeting in Japanese.

"*Ohayo,*" I said, smiling back. "Do you speak English?"

"English?" the man said with a thick accent. The man laughed and shook his head. "No. No English."

Then as an afterthought, he dredged his way through an obviously meager vocabulary and added, "Sorry."

I smiled at the man and said, "That's all right." I started looking over the wares being offered. There were a variety of colorful boxes, all of which seemed to contain different types of crackers or cookies. In a little glass-sided cabinet there were white buns of some sort made of rice dough and with some kind of filling, as well as cans of coffee. From the condensation on the inside of the cabinet, I could tell that these items were heated. I reached out and put my fingertips against the glass and felt the warmth.

I pointed at the cabinet and said, "I would like some coffee."

"Ah, hai, kah-fee" he said, reaching into the cabinet and bringing out a can of coffee.

I reached into my pocket and took out a handful of Japanese coins and held them out to the man. The man laughed, and peering at the coins, picked through them and selected a few. Then he handed me the can of coffee.

"Thank you," I said. "Arigato."

The man smiled back his gap-toothed grin and dipped his head. *"Do itashimashite,"* he answered.

I tore the aluminum tab off the can, went to a nearby bench, and sat down. The short contact with the man running the concession stand seemed to cheer me up. I thought that the man seemed like a happy soul, content with his life and with meeting people in the park. I wished my own life was not so complicated or filled with theft, murder, and six ancient blades.

The coffee was bitter but it was hot and satisfying, and I sipped at the can as I looked around the park. The trees were wearing a protective girdle of straw put on them by patient gardeners. Another sign that winter would be coming soon.

Down the path came a woman with a young child. The woman had a quilted coat and carried a shopping bag. The child looked six or seven. She had a red jacket, blue pants, and red rubber boots. Her hair was cut in the inevitable bangs, and bright eyes peered out from a round, cute face.

The woman walked over to the stand and bought one of the white rice buns and a foam cup of hot green tea. She took some napkins from the holder and walked over to the bench next to mine. They sat down and the woman offered the child a bite of the bun. The child nibbled at it and the mother picked up one of the napkins and dabbed at the child's mouth.

The child was at the age where she felt that her dignity was being infringed upon by this action and she pushed the napkin away. The mother lectured her for a few seconds, then handed the napkin over to the child, offering the bun for another bite. The child bit at the bun and this time wiped her own mouth. She said something to the mother, who reached into her shopping bag and pulled out a little plastic sack with a variety of toys in it.

The child reached in the sack and brought out a handkerchief which had its four corners tied together. The child undid the handkerchief and took out some pieces of plastic. They were brightly colored; red on one side and blue on the other.

I was fascinated by what kind of game this was. I noticed that the pieces were not all the same shape. Some were triangles, others were rectangles, and all of various sizes. The child dumped the pieces out on the bench and started arranging them so all the blue sides were up. Then she started moving the pieces around on the bench, placing the pieces next to each other, moving a piece from one side to the next and trying different combinations of the various forms. After a few minutes she said something to her mother, who looked at the pattern created by the child and nodded. Her mother went back to eating the bun as the child started rearranging the pieces.

I was intrigued, and when the child stopped and asked her mother to look, I stood up so I could get a clear picture of what the pattern was. I didn't want to intrude on her privacy, but I was intensely curious as to what the child was doing. The pieces of plastic had been pushed around, forming a head, stumpy triangular legs, and a little triangular tail. The pattern looked like it could be a cubist rendition of a horse or dog.

Once again the child started moving the pieces around, forming another pattern. She was aware that I was observing her, and acted nonchalant. Still, I think she liked the audience. This time she shoved the pieces around into what looked like a stylized tree. She didn't seem satisfied by that and moved the pieces around again.

Finally, after many rearrangements, she ended up with a triangular sail and the hull of a sailboat. Excitedly, she said something to the mother who looked down and nodded. The mother said something and the child flipped the pieces forming the sail over, changing the sail from blue to red, ending up with a blue-hulled boat with a red sail. The child seemed very pleased by this and as I watched I also became pleased.

I now had a way to unravel the secret of the sword blades.

The woman and the child finished their snack and moved on. I sat on the bench thinking about my solution to the problem, thinking through the computer techniques necessary to implement it. I took a scrap of paper and a pen from my pocket and tried sketching out my solution to see if I was right. I was so immersed that I didn't notice the two men walking up the path towards me.

As they came close, I glanced up and dropped the pen and paper. It was my two Yakuza pursuers, back again and mad. The tall one let fly with a fist to my head. I'd like to say my catlike re-flexes allowed me to avoid the blow, but the only cat my reflexes match is the chubby cartoon character Garfield. I did manage to move my head enough so the blow was just glancing, but it still hurt. A lot.

I tried twisting away but the tall guy grabbed the sleeve of my jacket so I couldn't run. Sitting on a bench is not the best fight-ing posture, but it does have the advantage of leaving your legs free to kick. Leaning over, I brought my right leg up between the legs of the shorter man. I connected hard, actually lifting him off the ground slightly. The enthusiasm for the fight drained from his face, along with most of his blood. He grabbed his crotch and doubled over.

The taller man was still active and threw another punch at me. I raised my arm to block it and was too slow. It hit me in the chest so hard that tears formed in my eyes. My assailant was too close to kick, so I tried to return the compliment with some punches of my own. He was able to easily block my off-balanced flailing and the SOB actually smiled at my attempts to defend myself. A gold front tooth glinted back at me through my tear-stained vi-sion.

He yanked at my jacket to get me in position for another shot at my head and managed to pull me off the bench. I fell to the earth with a hard thump to my shoulder. I knew what was prob-ably coming next, and I was already rolling away when he drew back his leg to kick me.

I managed to roll under the bench. I'd like to say my tormentor hurt his leg by kicking the bench, but he saw what I was doing and quickly crossed over to the other side of the bench to kick me from that side. Naturally, I reversed my direction and rolled under the bench the other way.

He barked an order to the shorter man and once again came around the bench to kick me. I changed direction again, rolling to put the bench between us for protection.

I don't know how long I could have kept up my impression of a rolling log, but I did know that as soon as the other thug re-covered from my kick to the gonads, my little game would be over. The tall guy would get on one side of the bench and the short one would get on the other. I'd be the piece of meat caught in the middle, and a stomping by two pissed-off gangsters is not how I pictured my trip to Japan ending.

The old man at the concession stand shouted something at the two thugs. The taller man once again came around the bench, forcing me to reverse direction. If I continued rolling, I'd never be able to get to my feet, but if I stopped rolling, I was sure I'd get a well-placed kick to my head or ribs.

The old man at the snack stand gave a second shout. From under the bench I could see the old man running from the stand towards the fight. He ran with a rolling, bowlegged gait, like a sailor on a tossing ship. Under other circumstances, it would have been comical. The old man was waving a knife. It was a short kitchen knife, probably used for slicing steamed buns. Despite the knife, the two Yakuza didn't take flight. Instead, the tall man quickly turned around and faced the approaching snack stand owner, growling something in Japanese. The old man slowed and then came to a stop, unsure about what he should do next.

The Yakuza then stared down at me. I looked up at him through the slats of the bench seat. He pointed a finger at me and said in heavily accented English, "Leave swords alone!" I blinked at him in surprise. I heard a noise behind me and glanced over my shoulder to see the shorter man starting to shuffle towards me, still clutching his crotch.

"Leave swords alone!" the tall man roared. I turned my attention to him and nodded vigorously. At my affirmative nod, the man grunted and repeated, "Leave swords alone." I nodded even more vigorously and said, "Hai."

The man nodded, looked at the smaller man and said something. The smaller man argued with the tall man, but the tall man seemed in charge. I don't know what they said, but I got a hint as the smaller man aimed a kick at me that landed on my hip instead of a more delicate part of my anatomy. The small guy wanted revenge.

Instead, he obeyed orders and the men started moving away from the bench, one man backing up and the other sort of shuffling as he continued to hold on to his crotch.

At the retreat of the thugs, the old man came up to the bench and peered down at me. He looked concerned and said something in Japanese.

Now that the shock of the attack was over, the pain was more noticeable and it was with great effort that I was able to roll out from underneath the bench and get to my feet. Despite the pain, I was more embarrassed than hurt.

"Arigatō," I said, thanking the old man. I tried to think of a more polite way of saying thank you, but the phrases wouldn't come to mind. "Arigatō," I repeated. The old man was saying something in Japanese, but I didn't understand.

"I'm staying at the hotel. Hotel," I said, pointing towards the Imperial. I couldn't remember the Japanese name for it. The old man nodded his understanding, and started to help me hobble towards the hotel. After a few steps, I stopped and shook off the old man's hand.

"No, thank you. I don't think I need you to help me get back to the hotel." I reached into my pocket and pulled out my wallet. I took out a fistful of Japanese bills and thrust them towards the old man. The old man shook his head no. He shoved the money back at me.

"Okay, I understand," I said. "Thank you for your help. Arigato." I hobbled towards the hotel with the old man staring after me.

During Vietnam, the federal government and U.S. Army spent a lot of money on me in an effort to turn me into a fighting machine. Because of a back injury, I spent less than three weeks in Vietnam, so the government didn't get its money's worth. Now, over twenty years later, I wish I had paid more attention to the hand-to-hand combat part of the training.

I stopped. Then I returned to the bench as fast as my sore body would let me so I could recover my note on how to solve the problem with the blades. Of course, I had no intention of keeping my promise to those SOBs to stay away from the swords.

21

I spent most of the morning sitting with Mariko at a Tokyo police station. This time, I got a couple of English-speaking officers who were sympathetic and patient. They said they'd bring
the two thugs in for questioning, but I decided not too much
would be done if they didn't pick up the two Yakuza before I
left Japan. I called *News Pop* to tell them where I was, and Buzz
Sugimoto came down to the station to help with translations and
for moral support. Mariko was stressed out by the encounter,
much more stressed than I. I had some bumps and bruises, but I
was more angry than fearful. Mariko, on the other hand, clung
to me so tightly that I had to ask her to back off a little, because
she was exacerbating my aches and pains. Lovers don't take too
kindly to their paramours being used as soccer balls.

When all the paperwork was completed, Mariko, Buzz, and
I left the police station. "You know what I don't understand?" I
said to him.

"What?"

"I thought the two Yakuza were going to tell me not to testify in Los Angeles, but instead the only thing they said was stay
away from the swords. I don't even know how they know I'm involved with the swords."

"Even Yakuza watch television," Mariko reminded me. "You
were on *News Pop* talking about the swords."

"But why they would care? They wanted me to promise I'd stop trying to solve the mystery of the swords."

"What did you say to them?" Sugimoto asked.

"What could I say? I said yes. It was either that or get kicked to death. But I gave them a Japanese yes."

"What do you mean?"

"Don't Japanese sometimes say yes to indicate that they understand, not that they agree?"

"That's true," Sugimoto said.

"I said yes because I understood, not because I agreed." I looked over at Mariko and she had a tight line for a mouth. If Sugimoto wasn't there I'm sure I would have gotten a real "stomach-to-stomach" talk about my intention to pursue this.

"So what are you going to do now?" Sugimoto asked.

"First, I want to take Mariko back to the hotel. There's no reason her sightseeing should be disturbed by this. Then, I want to get back to Nissan to talk to Mr. Kiyohara. I have an idea I want to run past him." The look on Mariko's face told me that sightseeing wasn't on her mind. I felt some guilt about going to Nissan, but I had to see if my idea for solving the puzzle of the swords would work. "Then afterwards, I'm going to see if I can figure out this Yakuza thing. If I could only talk to the head of the Sekiguchi-gummi, I might be able to understand what they want from me."

"I can arrange that," Sugimoto said.

"What?"

"If you want to talk to the head of the Sekiguchi-gummi, I can arrange it. We did a show about them a year ago because they sponsored a contest to encourage *sumi-e,* Japanese traditional ink painting."

"Organized crime sponsored a painting contest?"

"Junichi Sekiguchi considers himself a patron of the arts. In Japan, organized crime functions much more openly than in the United States. They still get involved in bad things, but they also have legitimate businesses they can use for things like sponsoring a contest. I'm pretty sure I can get you in to see him if you really want to talk to him. Do you want to do it today?"

"No, tomorrow. I want to make some arrangements first. Right now, I'd like to talk to Kiyohara-san."

Within an hour I was facing Mr. Kiyohara across a metal table in a cramped conference room in the Nissan building. Excited, I launched into my solution to the problem of the blades.

"We use brute force."

Kiyohara-san was puzzled by my statement, so I continued. "When you come right down to it, the solution is pretty simple. We've got six sword blades we're dealing with and I think they fit together to form a map. The question is how do they fit together? This question is made harder by the fact that one of the blades is missing. I've been trying to come up with some elegant way of deducing how the blades fit together and what the map looks like, but actually this isn't necessary.

"Although the problem looks impossibly hard, when you start moving the swords around to find all the patterns, you discover there are just twelve possibilities. That's all. Are you familiar with the Japanese children's game with the different shaped pieces of plastic? The one where kids move the pieces around until they make recognizable shapes?"

Puzzled, Kiyohara said, "Yes."

"By computer we're going to do something similar with the patterns on the blades. I'll explain the details, but the important thing to keep in mind is that there are twelve, and only twelve, ways the blades can fit together, even when you account for the blade we don't know about."

"Now I'm confused," Kiyohara said. "How can there only be twelve possibilities?"

I picked up a pencil and a sheet of paper. "Watch. From the numbers on the tangs we know where three blades fit. These are blades one, three and six. That's Sonoda-san's blade, the blade from Rotterdam, and my blade. We know the patterns on two of the other blades, and of course one blade is missing. Let's call the missing blade X, and the two patterns we do have A and B. The problem is how to fit them together so we can match this pattern to a map of Japan."

"Let's assume that the missing blade is the second blade. Let's label the New York blade A and assume it's the fourth blade. The Tokyo blade, which we'll label B, then becomes the fifth one. This is the pattern we would have."

On the sheet of paper I wrote, "1 X 3 A B 6."

"Now that may or may not be the real pattern formed on the blades. For instance, perhaps we have the New York blade and the Tokyo blade switched around. That would give us this pattern."

I labeled a column two and I wrote, "1 X 3 B A 6."

"Those are the only two variations if the missing blade is the second blade. But what if the missing blade isn't the second blade? What if it's the fourth blade? Well, we end up with two more patterns."

I quickly drew the patterns on the paper. "And if the missing blade is the fifth blade we end up with this pattern." I drew the remaining two patterns. I pointed down to the sheet of paper with the six patterns.

one	two	three	four	five	six
1	1	1	1	1	1
X	X	A	B	A	B
3	3	3	3	3	3
A	B	X	X	B	A
B	A	B	A	X	X
6	6	6	6	6	6

"See, there are only six possibilities here. If we reverse the order so the numbers on the tangs go from six to one, instead of one to six, that doubles the combinations. That's still only twelve patterns, regardless of which blade is missing and what order the Tokyo blade and the New York blade fit into the pattern. We don't have to know which is the right pattern. All we have to do is enter all twelve into a computer program that will try to match each pattern to the Nissan digitized map of Japan.

"I know a digitized map is kept as a series of numbers, very much like the numbers you showed me for the photo enhancement. For instance, a section of a digitized map might look like this." I took a piece of paper and a pencil and wrote:

```
0 4 4 4 4 4 4 4 4 4
4 0 4 4 4 6 6 6 6 4
4 0 4 4 6 6 6 6 6 6
4 4 0 4 6 6 6 6 6 6
4 4 0 4 4 4 4 4 4 4
```

Kiyohara stayed silent, but as soon as I put down my pencil he said, "What's that?"

"It's a simplified drawing of a digitized map. For instance, zero could be water, so the string of zeros on the left side of the diagram could be a river. The number 4 could be flat farmland, and 6 could be foothills. If we knew the patterns on the six blades we could create a similar map looking at temples, rivers, and mountains. The temples and villages shown on the blades may have moved or disappeared, but it's not likely that something like a mountain will vanish, so we're bound to have landmarks that will line up. By computer we can match the blades' map to the Nissan Japan map.

"After four hundred years, we're not going to get a perfect match, but we can calculate how close a match we get and review those portions of Japan which give us as close a fit as possible. We can actually eliminate a lot of geography. We're probably looking at a very small portion of the main island of Honshu, probably centered around Osaka castle and the surrounding countryside. Osaka was the stronghold of the Toyotomi, wasn't it?"

Kiyohara nodded.

"If we had the pattern on the blades," I continued, "the actual matching of the blades to your map would be easy. Our problem is we don't have all the blades and we also don't know how they fit together. The solution to those problems is that we don't have to come up with an answer."

"What?"

"Because one-sixth of the map is missing, theoretically the best match we could come up with is five-sixths, or eighty-three percent. If we had the landmarks on all six blades I suppose we could match things one hundred percent, but I'm betting that starting with an eighty-three percent match will be good enough. We can't match perfectly, but we can narrow down the search, and maybe there are other clues that can help us."

"How will we know the scale to use with the map on the blades?"

"We've got several mountains shown on the blades. If we get a match on mountain locations, we just adjust the scale to match the distance between the mountains on the digitized map. Then we look to see if things like rivers, temples, and villages align."

"I see," Kiyohara said. "So there are only twelve possible patterns."

"That's right."

"And instead of trying to figure out which is the right pattern, we'll just try to match all patterns, using mountains as landmarks to set the proper scale."

"That's right. That's the beauty of it. By using the computer, we can try all combinations. That would be difficult to do manually, but the computer will grind away trying every combination of blade pattern to every geographic location to see if it gets a match. We can even measure how close each pattern fits. We can come up with something like a percentage scale that will measure how close each of the patterns fits to the current geography of the area. It will chew up a lot of Nissan's computer power, but by switching things around and trying different combinations we might come up with the answer."

Kiyohara tapped the diagram with the various combinations. "This is pretty good. You just swapped things around, trying different combinations. How did you come up with it?"

I smiled. "I was trying to find some elegant solution and I was totally stumped. But after I saw it was simply a matter of shuffling the patterns around and trying every possible combination, I realized that this whole problem was actually child's play."

22

The headquarters of the Sekiguchi-gummi was near Tokyo's Tsujiki Fish Market, in a relatively modest neighborhood of three- and four-story buildings. It was in a modern four-story office building that looked neat and clean. There were no signs on the front, but there was some kind of logo on the front door of the building done in gold. It was a circle with three bars and a dot.

It seemed peculiar to me that a crime family would have an office, but I guess in some American cities organized crime uses bars and restaurants for its headquarters, and everyone in the neighborhood knows it. Sugimoto had offered to come with me but I turned him down. His English skills would have been handy, but I didn't trust him. I might be paranoid, but I didn't know what his past relationship with the Sekiguchi-gummi was, so I didn't want him coming along to muddy up the waters. Besides, I had arranged for my own companion.

We walked through the front door of the building. In the modest lobby there was a desk and a young man in his twenties was sitting there to act as a receptionist. He was studying some kind of newspaper. It looked like the horse-racing forms we have in the United States, except this paper had pictures of small outboard motor boats that seemed to be racing each other around some kind of circular pond with a grandstand. Many Asians like to gamble and it looked like this guy was selecting his picks for races to be held that day.

He didn't bother looking up at us until we approached his desk. Then he looked up from his paper and continued to look up and up and further up. He more or less ignored me, but since I was standing next to Gary Apia, I could see where I might be lost in the shadow of Gary's seven-foot, five-hundred-pound frame. The man sat there with an open mouth.

When I asked Gary to accompany me, he had given me a quick "Sure, bruddah."

"Before you agree, let me explain what's happening." I told him about my involvement with the Sekiguchi-gummi in Los Angeles and what I wanted to accomplish with my visit. I also told him of my run-in with the Yakuza in Hibiya Park. "You might not want to get involved with these guys," I said.

He laughed. "Those kinda guys are always sniffing around the rikishi, looking for a tip on who to bet on. They don't scare me. Let's go for broke."

That Hawaiian what-the-hell attitude never sounded sweeter to my ears, and now that we were actually in the lobby of the Sekiguchi-gummi building, I was glad to be standing next to him. He was wearing a blue kimono, and his hair was in a simplified version of the elaborate, slicked down hairstyle he wore for sumo wrestling. He told me he was required to dress this way by the association that runs sumo in Japan, and he looked very much like a seventeenth century warrior, instead of a modern athlete. It was hardly the dress for inconspicuous sleuthing, but I wanted to call as much attention to us as possible. If something happened to us, I wanted plenty of people noticing that we went into this building.

Gary, in broken Japanese, announced who we were and why we were there. No response. Gary repeated his request for us to see the head of the Sekiguchi-gummi, then he looked at me and said, "Dis guy must be dumb. My Japanese is bad, but he should know your name and why we're here."

I personally thought that sitting in slack-jawed amazement was probably a pretty good response when confronted with Gary's imposing presence for the first time. The guy acting as a receptionist must have decided it wasn't a wise policy to irritate the giant, because he finally picked up a phone and started talking in rapid Japanese.

In a few moments a pinched-faced, middle-aged woman came into the lobby. When she saw Gary her eyebrows raised slightly, but otherwise she gave no indication that it was at all unusual to have a kimono-clad mountain standing there. She looked at me and said, "Mr. Tanaka, I'm Mr. Sekiguchi's private secretary. He asked me to bring you to his office. I'm so very sorry, but I think we might have a problem getting your friend up to his office."

"What do you mean?" Gary said, his eyebrows narrowing suspiciously.

"Please come with me," she said. She took us out of the lobby and down a short hall. At the end of the hall was a tiny elevator, which would normally only hold two or three people. It was hard to imagine how Gary would fit into the elevator.

"I don't like dis," Gary said.

I thought about ancient Japanese castles with winding entrances and narrow passages which were designed to break up formations of enemy troops. I wondered if the elevator had the same function.

"Why don't you wait for me, Gary?" I said. "With you here I don't think anything will happen."

"Are you sure, bruddah?"

"Pretty sure. Just don't wander too far away."

"No sweat, bruddah." He looked at the secretary and said, "Will you do da translating for him?" I smiled at this. Even I could tell that Gary's linguistic skills in Japanese were rudimentary, at best. But still, he spoke a lot more conversational Japanese than I could muster.

"Mr. Sekiguchi speaks English, so I'm certain there'll be no problems with Mr. Tanaka and Mr. Sekiguchi speaking to each other."

The woman and I crowded into the small elevator. She pressed the button for the fourth floor and we started ascending. I was once in an elevator in New York City, in an old building on Bleecker Street, that was smaller than two phone booths. You could hardly inhale, but the sign on the wall said the maximum capacity was thirteen. I don't know if Japanese elevator companies have an equally perverse sense of humor, but the elevator we were in was so small that crowding more than three into it would probably constitute some kind of sexual encounter.

When we got to the fourth floor, the door opened and I was stunned.

The elevator opened into a small lobby. While the public lobby downstairs was austere and rather cheap looking, the lobby up here was positively opulent. The rug was a thick blue wool and the walls were beautifully paneled with dark and light woods inlaid in a geometric pattern of rectangles.

In the center of the lobby was a large desk made of wood so dark it almost looked black. The secretarial chair and word processor made me conclude this was the command station for my guide. Hanging on the wall behind the desk was a scroll painting. I don't know that much about Japanese painting, but this one looked very old and very elegant. It was a painting of a monkey sitting in the bottom corner of the scroll, looking up. In the upper corner of the painting, about six feet from the monkey's face, there was a tiny butterfly. The huge expanse of white space between the monkey and the butterfly was pristine and effective. In Japanese painting they say that the white space is often as important as the brush strokes, and in this particular composition that was certainly true. The white space made you realize how far above the monkey the beauty of the butterfly was.

On the secretary's desk was an ikebana flower arrangement. It was a single iris, a long green leaf, and two small white chrysanthemums. Each piece of the arrangement was in perfect harmony and balance with the other. Very elegant and very much in keeping with the lobby.

The secretary walked over to one of the wooden panels and gently pushed, revealing that the panel was a hidden door. Once again I thought about old Japanese castles, which often had secret panels or passageways so that the lord of the castle could escape in case of unexpected attack. The secretary stood to one side and bowed in order to usher me in to Sekiguchi's office.

In Japan, adoption of adults is not uncommon. Sometimes when a young man marries into a family with no male heir, he will agree to take his wife's name for his own in order to continue the wife's family name. Kabuki actors and woodblock artists also commonly adopt their favorite pupils to pass on their name. Because of this custom, I wasn't sure of the relationship that Mr. Sekiguchi had with the Sekiguchi-gummi crime family. I didn't know if he was the founder of this family, some relative of the founder, or someone who had been adopted into the family and taken the Sekiguchi name. My purpose was not the genealogy of Japanese crime families, but still I was curious about how one got to be the head of a Japanese Mafia family. I suspect it involves acts and decisions that are pretty grim.

I thought the lobby was pretty posh, but it was nothing compared to the actual office. Sekiguchi's office was designed to impress, and with me it did its job. It was a long rectangular room with a high ceiling. You entered at the far end of the rectangle and sitting at the other end, in splendid isolation, was a massive rosewood desk with a couple of black leather chairs set in front of it. The walls on either side of the office were pierced with small alcoves. In the alcoves were pieces of pottery or small Japanese paintings, each illuminated by its own light. These alcove walls were also paneled in rosewood and this, combined with the dark carpet, gave the office the feeling of a somber cathedral.

Sitting behind the desk was a tiny wizened man in a gray suit. On his desk were no papers, so he looked like a small statue set in a sea of wine-colored wood. As I waded through the thick carpet towards the desk, I was reminded of the scene in the *Wizard of Oz* where Dorothy and her companions are walking in the great hall of the Emerald City to approach the wizard. They're so in awe that they're shaking as they walk.

My confidence was strained by having to leave Gary behind and by the obvious wealth and opulence behind the facade of a modest building. This office was designed to achieve an effect, and that effect was intimidation. Because of that, I did something I normally wouldn't do, especially with a Japanese national I was meeting for the first time. I marched down the length of the office and flopped down into a chair without being invited.

That, of course, was rude, and rudeness is something usually avoided with strangers in Japanese culture. But rudeness is also sometimes used to establish relative social positions. To me, the layout of Sekiguchi's office, including the long march to his desk, was designed to make you feel like a supplicant, inching your way towards the dais of a shógun. I was ticked off at this man, and my aching head and bruised hip reminded me why I was angry. I wasn't going to let something like a clever layout of his office beat me down.

Sekiguchi stared at me impassively as I flopped down into the chair. As an American, I suppose he expected me to be too familiar and rude. I wanted him to know that I understood the proper protocol to follow in this meeting and I had chosen to ignore it, but there wasn't a way to actually say it. The head looking back at me was almost bald, with wisps of silver hair still clinging to the sides. His pate was freckled with brown spots. The eyes were as hard as two black pearls. He was probably in his late sixties, but his bearing was still erect and as stiff as a weathered pine standing on top of a mountainside.

Without a preamble, Sekiguchi spoke. "Because this meeting was arranged on short notice, I can only give you fifteen minutes. Why do you want to speak to me?"

My apprehensions and fears dissolved. I fought to keep from giggling. Not because of nervousness, but because the man behind the desk, the head of the Sekiguchi-gummi crime family, talked like Marlon Brando in *The Godfather*. He didn't have a Sicilian accent, but he tended to mumble his words in a low whisper. I don't know if he always talked this way or if it was an affectation picked up after he saw the movie, but the effect on me was not sinister or menacing at all. It was comical.

I regained my composure and a bit of my cockiness with the unexpected comic relief. "Thank you for your time. I realize this is on short notice and I appreciate you seeing me."

The man nodded.

"Do you know who I am?" I asked.

"I understand you're from California and that you're an American and that you've appeared on the Japanese television show *News Pop*."

"I was also responsible for getting your son arrested."

Mr. Sekiguchi stared at me expressionless. I would hate to

play poker with him. Trying to get a response from him, I pushed on. "I can see that my involvement with your son's case could be upsetting. That's why I wanted to meet with you to talk to you about why you're trying to harm me."

Once again he sat silent and motionless. I thought about the two thugs chasing me in Tokyo and my amusement over Mr. Sekiguchi's Godfatherlike voice disappeared. I forced myself to relax. Showing anger would be showing weakness. I raised my eyebrows slightly and waited.

I had already used up a couple of my allotted fifteen minutes. If Mr. Sekiguchi wanted to sit there in silence for the remaining thirteen minutes, then I was quite content to sit there in silence, too. I wasn't going to beg or plead with him. I'm not above begging or pleading, it's just that I figured with this man those tactics wouldn't work.

Finally, after a silence of several minutes, Mr. Sekiguchi sat back in his chair. Studying me carefully, he said, "What makes you think I want to harm you?"

"Several times now, two men identified by the police as members of the Yakuza have chased me. It's been the same two men so I know it's not an accident. Yesterday they caught me in Hibiya Park and roughed me up. Since the only connection I've ever had with the Yakuza is through your son, I think their interest in pursuing me is because of what happened between your son and me in California."

Once again Sekiguchi remained impassive and almost immobile. I reacted by settling back in the chair, as if his silence was an invitation to make myself more at home. Finally, Sekiguchi broke the silence and said, "Toshi is my youngest son and one that I have indulged over the years. I'm afraid that does not make me a very good father. I sent him to school in the United States and helped set him up in business in California in the hope that the new climate and responsibility would help him to grow up.

"Like every Japanese father, I'm very concerned about my children. But in the case of what happened in California, Toshi made several mistakes and he must pay for them. I don't view the punishment he'll receive as something which must be paid because he has done wrong. In my view he has not done wrong. But he made many mistakes and those mistakes can be serious. In the life we have chosen, if a man is to be a leader, he must be careful and he must be thoughtful. Perhaps because I have indulged him, Toshi is not very careful and sometimes he is not very thoughtful.

"The time he will spend in an American prison will allow him to grow more reflective and more serious about his life and about our business. Our California lawyers tell me that he'll not be in prison for a very long time. Actually quite less than the five years he spent graduating from USC. I think the education he will get from getting caught because he was careless will be much more valuable than the time he spent in college.

"Because of these feelings I have no personal grudge against you and do not wish you harmed. In fact, until this interview, I did not know who you were or what your involvement was with my son. I don't know why other Yakuza would want to chase you, but whatever the reason, it has nothing to do with the Sekiguchi-gummi."

He sat back in his chair and his hand disappeared under the desktop. For a brief second I thought he had set me up so that he could reach under the desk for a gun or some other weapon, but when the secretary popped through the door behind me a few seconds later, I realized he had simply reached for some kind of hidden buzzer to summon her. I knew the interview was over and stood up.

"And you have no interest in the Toyotomi blades?" I asked as a parting shot.

He was used to hiding his thoughts and gave me no response, but I thought I detected a slight flash of puzzlement in his eyes. I felt like I had just driven to the Tokyo Match Company.

In the story about the tourist and the matchbook, the taxi driver ignored the hotel logo on the front of the matches and focused on the name of the match company. It was a plausible but wrong assumption. I had done the same thing.

Junichi Sekiguchi could be lying. I'm sure in his business he's learned to lie rather well. But what he said rang true, and I was sure I saw surprise when I asked him about the Toyotomi blades.

When I identified the two men, the police said they were involved with right-wing politics and the Nippon Tokkotai. But because I saw no connection between me and Japanese politics, I ignored that association. Instead, I jumped on the Yakuza connection that the two men shared, and just focused on that, assuming the Sekiguchi-gummi was interested in me. I still couldn't understand why a Japanese political group was interested in me, but the warning in the park provided me with the thing that linked us: the swords.

I met Gary in the lobby and we walked out of the Sekiguchi-gummi headquarters together.

"You weren't up there long, bruddah," Gary said.

"About fifteen minutes. It was long enough to learn that I've been barking up the wrong tree."

"What you mean?"

"I mean I'm stumped about why those two guys have been chasing me all over Tokyo. I don't think the connection is the

Yakuza anymore. It involves some kind of radical Japanese political group, but I don't understand why they're interested in me, except that it involves the swords in some way." I stopped and looked up at Gary. "You're not Japanese, but you are from the islands. Do you know what *ongiri* is?"

"Sure, dat's da kine obligation, right?"

"Yes. It means I'm in your debt now because of what you've just done for me. You didn't have to go in there with me. It could have been dangerous and you've put yourself out for me."

"Hey, it's no big deal, bruddah. I wanted to see what dis place is like. I couldn't even fit in da elevator. Ain't no sweat 'bout me helping you. Don't get no pilikia wrinkles over it."

It took me a second to translate pilikia to worry. In its way, Hawaiian Pidgin was sometimes as foreign to me as Japanese. "It wasn't just nothing. Look, if there's anyway I can help you in the future, you just call me." I took a slip of paper from my pocket. "This is my phone number and address in Los Angeles. If there's anything I can ever do to help you, just call. I owe you now, big time."

"Naah," Gary said, but he took the paper and put it in his pocket.

We went to the van we came in and Gary climbed into the back, pretty much filling up the space there. I climbed into the passenger seat next to the driver, and Gary said, "You want to go to the hotel?"

"If you could drop me off at the Nissan building in the Ginza that would be great. I have an appointment there this morning."

"No sweat." Gary gave some instructions in halting Japanese to the driver and we quickly made our way from the Tsujiki district to the nearby Ginza.

As soon as I got to the Nissan building I knew there was going to be good news. There was a camera crew from *News Pop,* as well as Junko, waiting for me. Junko informed me that Nissan had asked the crew to come down and videotape the meeting we were about to have. No one calls in a camera crew to admit defeat.

In the lobby I not only met Kiyohara, but Kiyohara's boss. Another good sign. Now that the work was successful, the big boss wanted to show up for a little airtime. He made a flowery speech in the lobby to me, all in Japanese. I smiled and nodded appreciatively, even though I didn't have the slightest idea what he was saying. Junko's terse translation was that he was saying he was glad that Nissan could apply its technical prowess to help solve this mystery. I was glad, too, but frankly I was more interested in seeing what the results were. Even I could figure out that the ten-minute speech in the lobby would be reduced to a five-second clip of us shaking hands if it made it to the show.

They took us up to the seventh floor of the building and into a beautiful conference room, complete with wood paneling and artwork on the walls. The other conference rooms we had met in were austere and crowded hovels, but there's nothing like the remorseless little glass eye of the television camera to cause people to show their best. The TV crew set up in a few minutes and we were soon rolling tape again. Around the wood conference table were the members of Kiyohara's team, all polished and dressed up in their best clothes. They seemed to have happy expressions on their faces, and I was dying to see if my reaction to their results matched their obvious pleasure.

But first the big boss gave another five-minute speech in front of the assembled team and the newly set up camera. At last Junko told me that he was turning it over to Kiyohara to explain the results. "Finally," I muttered under my breath while still keeping a smile on my face. Both Junko and Kiyohara, who were close enough to hear me, smiled.

"You must be anxious to see the results of our efforts to match the patterns on the blades with our computerized map of Japan," Kiyohara said. He reached over and an assistant handed him four large sheets of paper. "These are maps with the results of our search. We had four areas that had a match of over sixty percent. With only five of the six blades available, the best match we could theoretically come up with was eighty-three percent, so we considered anything over sixty percent to be a very good match.

"We did further research and we discovered that two of the maps matched against temples that were built after 1650." He grabbed two of the papers and moved them to one side. "Since the treasure must have been hidden before the final defeat of the Toyotomi in the early 1600s, we reasoned that they couldn't be the temples shown on the blades. We know from the dates on the handles the blades were forged in 1614. That leaves us with these two possible locations." He shoved the remaining two pieces of paper over to me. They were computer maps drawn on a plotter. Modern roads and mountains were drawn in color on the maps, along with the location of major buildings and temples. Superimposed on each map was a red pattern of temples, mountains, and streams, which represented the patterns found on the blades. The match between the red blade patterns and the map features was not exact, but they were both remarkably close.

"This map is a location to the east of Osaka. This second map is to the north of Osaka, near Lake Biwa. Lake Biwa is now a resort area, but it's also an ancient part of Japan. Hideyoshi Toyotomi built or repaired bridges and temples there, including Enryaku-ji temple, which is one of the temples we matched on the map.

"Both areas seem very good prospects. One is close to the Toyotomi's main castle in Osaka and the other is near an ancient place in Japan with ties to the Toyotomis."

"This is great," I said, and I continued with effusive praise for Nissan, Kiyohara, Kiyohara's team, and even Kiyohara's boss. What the hell, I thought, I'd include the old windbag along with the deserving. Kiyohara returned the compliment, praising my ideas on how to match the blade patterns with one blade missing and how to try all the possible different sequences that the blades could fit together. All this mutual praise was part Japanese custom, but it was also heartfelt, at least on my part. I was so much further ahead of where I thought I'd be when I accepted the challenge and I wouldn't look like an idiot on the upcoming show. My ass was on the line and now it was saved. Or, in Japanese terms, I had saved face. I don't know which anatomical part is correct, but I was pretty happy from top to bottom.

As the *News Pop* crew was packing up I asked Kiyohara-san, "How did you handle that mysterious line on my blade?"

"We didn't know what it was, so we just ignored it."

I thanked Kiyohara again and walked over to Junko, who was supervising the camera crew's breakdown of the lights.

"So what's next?"

"I suppose we'll scout out the locations on the two maps and send camera crews to get film if we think it warrants it. Why?"

"I'd like to go with whoever looks over the site at Lake Biwa."

"You know something," Junko said.

"Yes, I think I do."

"Another hunch?"

"More than a hunch. I think it's likely that the treasure is buried at some place indicated on the third or fourth blade, because that's the center of the map. The third blade has some type of rock in the shape of an M in the dead center of the blade, so if that's accurate, I think we can pinpoint the probable location of the treasure pretty closely."

"But why do you want to go to Lake Biwa?"

"You know that long line on my blade? The one we were trying to figure out?"

"Yes."

"Kiyohara-san didn't use that in his computer match because he couldn't figure out what it was, either, but now that I've seen the Lake Biwa map I think the line represents the lake shore. Kiyohara said the Toyotomi were active at Lake Biwa?"

"Yes they were. There are several shrines and bridges built by Hideyoshi at Lake Biwa. I'm not a historian, but I have visited the lake and know that much."

"The Osaka site is closer to the Toyotomi base of operations, but if I was going to hide an emergency cache of treasure, I'd want to place it away from my main base, not next to it."

Junko got excited. "Look," she said, "can you do me a favor?"

"What is it?"

"Don't tell anyone else what you think about the Lake Biwa site. I want to be the one who goes there, and if Buzz finds out that it's likely to be the treasure site, he'll pull strings to get me sent to Osaka while he goes treasure hunting. I want to make sure the reverse happens."

W e piled out of the Nissan Patrol as soon as Junko stopped the engine. The Jeep-like Patrol might be fine for acting like a mountain goat, but it was not my idea of the ideal vehicle for the long drive from Tokyo to Lake Biwa. Mariko and I were plenty glad to escape the confines of the vehicle to work out the kinks from our bodies.

The producers of *News Pop* had been ecstatic over the results obtained. They generously offered to pay for Mariko to go with me to Lake Biwa, along with Junko. The plan was for us to scout locations for a day. Then Nagahara-san would show up to film some location shots and an on-the-scene promo. Yukiko-chan was doing the same thing with Sugimoto at the Osaka location. Then the network planned to promote the hell out of a special *News Pop* show that centered around the blades and the treasure. Junko told me the producers were positively giddy over the ratings possibilities for the show.

The four of us were staying at a small village near the center of the map. The village was several kilometers north of the main town of Ostu and had a small main street of bars and a couple of clubs that catered to vacationing tourists. We were staying at a *ryokan*, or Japanese-style inn, that was located on a side street off the main road. I was surprised to see that the inn looked very much like a farmer's hut and wondered what I was getting myself into after the pampered care of the Imperial.

The ryokan had a low tile roof and a porch made of a dark, weather-stained wood. In front of the inn were sliding shōji screens with a band of clear panels halfway up the screen. A little wooden sign with Japanese characters hung near the door. We walked up to the shōji screen and slid it back. Junko stuck her head into the opening and said, *"Sumimasen,"* or excuse me.

There was a scurrying of feet inside the inn and a short, square-faced woman wearing a brown kimono greeted us. The woman stood about five feet tall and her hair was pulled back into a glossy bun. She bowed and she and Junko exchanged greetings. They talked for a few minutes and the woman bowed again, motioning for us to walk into the entryway of the inn.

"What about the bags?" I asked.

"She says her son will get them from the car," Junko said, handing over the car keys to the woman.

"This is the only Japanese-style inn in this village," Junko said. "We were lucky to get rooms here." She sat down on a bench near the door and took off her shoes. The woman took slippers out from a bookcaselike shelf near the side of the entrance and handed them to Junko. Mariko and I followed suit.

Junko and the woman talked for a few more minutes, then Junko said to us, "She says we're going to share the best rooms in the inn. Shows you the power of television."

We followed the woman to a door at the back of the lobby. When I walked through the door I was surprised to see that we were outside and there was a covered walkway leading to the next structure.

Junko talked to the woman as she scurried past us in the hallway to lead us into the next structure and to our room. "She says that her family has owned this inn for about one hundred twenty years. The original building, the one with the lobby, is actually about three hundred years old. Over the years, her family has bought up surrounding houses and added the passageways and that's how they've been able to expand. She says our rooms will open up into a private garden."

The woman led us further down a passageway and stopped, sliding back a shōji screen. Junko entered, followed by Mariko and me. We were standing in a plain, rectangular room of wood, paper, and grass tatami mats. The woman crossed the room and opened up the shōjis on the back wall. Before us was a beautiful miniature garden of dark rock, bamboo, and green moss.

Junko sucked in a breath of surprise and walked over to the open shōji. "It's beautiful, isn't it," she said.

I walked over and looked out. The garden was no more than twelve feet across and four feet deep. In one corner was a grove of bamboo, and in the middle was a sloping hillside covered with a thick blanket of moss. Jagged rocks were artfully arranged on the hillside, giving the illusion of looking out on a vista with distant mountains. The moss had a golden haze from the late afternoon sunshine, and it formed a rolling carpet around the rocks and up around the base of the bamboo.

Mariko said, "This is going to be great. I'm really glad we came. Even if we don't find any treasure, this will be a wonderful vacation for us. Should we tip the lady?"

Junko shook her head. "No. Her name is Mrs. Sakurai and we certainly shouldn't tip her. The tip will be added to our bill as a service charge. We should, of course, thank her." Which she proceeded to do, bowing and saying her thanks in Japanese. I could see Mariko didn't like the tone of Junko's correction.

I gave an awkward bow and said, "Arigatō," which elicited some giggles from Mrs. Sakurai. She said something to Junko. "She said she thinks you're really cute," Junko said. "Mariko, Sakurai-san told me she has daughters as well as sons working here. Watch out!"

Mariko sighed. "I don't see what the attraction is, but I'm used to defending my investment in this guy." That seemed a warning as much as a statement.

Mrs. Sakurai left and Junko walked over to the wall and slid back one panel, revealing a row of shelves with pillows, linens, and blankets. "We've got two rooms, a tatami room and a Western-style room. I'll take the Western-style room, if you don't mind, and you can have the tatami room. The tatami room has a private bath with a Japanese-style o-furo bathtub." She reached onto a shelf and held up a gray and white kimono, "We also have yukatas. They're summer kimonos. Inns like this usually provide them for guests to wear, so they can be comfortable. It's a little bit chilly for them, but I suppose we can increase the heat in the room, or I can call Mrs. Sakurai and ask her to send us some flannel ones, instead."

"This room has central heating?"

"Yes. She said she had it added to this wing and the main entry wing. See, all the comforts of home. It just looks old-fashioned. What more could you want? You're the king surrounded by two queens."

I looked around, "Well, I could ask for a bedroom, and for that matter a bed."

"Sakurai-san's son will show up with the luggage any minute and we can eat dinner. We'll have the dinner brought to our room, ryokan style. After that, someone will come and lay out the futons for you. Futons are sort of a padded mat. They roll right out on top of the tatamis. I think you'll find them comfortable. I'll be relaxing in a Western-style bed."

Ryokan living was a combination of camping out and being treated like Japanese royalty. We sat on cushions on the tatami floor as our dinner was served to us in the room by Mrs. Sakurai and one of her daughters. They didn't go through all the folderol of the Kori-Mizu in Kyoto, but the atmosphere was warm, the food was delicious, and we had a good time. After dinner there was a lull in the conversation because I think we all realized we had a long evening to kill until we could start scouting treasure locations with the coming of the next day.

25

Junko announced, "I'm going to take a shower and then I'm going to bed."

"Are you sure? Mariko and I are going to play some *hanafuda* after our bath. You're welcome to join us. We're going to play for loose change, and I'm always willing to have another source of money in the game."

"Can you get hanafuda?"

"Mrs. Sakurai will bring us some hanafuda. I managed to ask during dinner," Mariko said.

Hanafuda are Japanese playing cards. The name means flower cards. They're printed on tiny pasteboards, about two and a half inches by one inch. They have suites with things like the moon, plum blossoms, bush clover, pine trees, or maple leaves. Some of the card designs are quite beautiful, with things like deer in a maple forest, birds flying across a full moon, or irises in the rain.

"No, I really am very tired and I want to go to sleep. We should get an early start tomorrow," Junko said.

"Okay. If you're going to use a Western-style shower, then Mariko and I will use the Japanese o-furo. We'll see you in the morning for breakfast. Good night."

"Good night," Junko said.

When Junko left, Mariko and I went into the Japanese-style bathroom. The Japanese o-furo tub was a big wooden affair set along one side of the room. The tub was already full and there seemed to be a constant stream of hot water flowing through it from an opening set in the tub's side. Two benches faced each other in the tub, so it was designed for cozy couples.

I know about o-furos, but I had never actually been in one. I have some non-Japanese friends whose daughter married a Japanese national. When they went to Japan to visit their in-laws, they were offered use of Japanese-style bath first, which is the place of honor. When they were finished, they pulled the plug, draining all the water, which is a social faux pas because it takes so long to heat up the enormous tubs. This mistake was never mentioned by their in-laws, of course.

This difference in bath customs can cause problems in the other direction, too. When my friends had their Japanese in-laws visit them, the Japanese parents of their son-in-law were offered the use of an upstairs bathroom in my friend's two-story house. This bathroom is tiled, just like most Japanese bathrooms. Unlike most Japanese bathrooms, however, it doesn't have a drain in the middle of the floor, a detail the Japanese in-laws didn't notice. My friends were sitting in their living room when they noticed their stairs had turned into an indoor waterfall. Rushing upstairs, they found water flowing from under the bathroom door. Their Japanese in-laws had used the handheld shower massager to clean themselves off before getting into the tub, Japanese style, and the water had caused a flood.

There must have been foreign tourists staying at the ryokan before, because I noticed with amusement that the drain plug on the bath had a little brass padlock on it, making it impossible for a guest to drain the bath. Because the bathwater is not drained between users, it's tremendously bad etiquette to enter a Japanese tub dirty. I sat on a small plastic stool next to Mariko and soaped myself up and rinsed myself off using a small bucket and wash cloth. The water from this cleansing went into a drain set in the bathroom floor. The erotic possibilities of soaping up Mariko entered my head, and I helped her get clean with verve. Any visions of hot tub orgies I may have had, however, diminished as soon as I started to get into the o-furo.

The water in a hot tub is pleasantly warm, but the water in an o-furo is scalding. It took me a good five minutes to lower myself into it, inching down into the steaming water by slow degrees. Mariko was able to plunge into the water in just a few seconds.

"I feel like the featured dish in a Louisiana crab boil," I complained.

"Yeah, but after you get used to it, you'll find the hot water tremendously relaxing. I could see falling asleep in here."

"If you did you'd be in the burn ward of the local hospital."

"It's not that bad."

"That's a matter of opinion. There seems to be a constant stream of scalding water coming into this tub."

"You're supposed to like it. It's cultural."

"In case you haven't noticed, culturally I'm American, not Japanese."

As soon as I said that I realized that I meant more than just my preferences in bath water. From the moment I came to Japan, when the customs agent spoke Japanese to me, I was trying to sort out what it meant to return to the land of my ancestors. I felt strangely comfortable in Japan. Sights, sounds, customs, and the faces of the people had a resonance with me that reminded me I come from Japanese stock. But this was an ease that came from preserved memories, not from actually fitting in. Foundations of culture transcend race, and I realized that my culture is American.

No matter how much interest I might have in Japan, no matter how much I learned about it from books and documentaries and even visits, I would never be Japanese. That might seem obvious, but like Buzz Sugimoto, who was dumbfounded when I pointed out that his symbols of rebellion over Japan becoming too Westernized were actually Western, I achieved resolution from a statement which should have been clearly apparent. No matter how uncomfortable I may sometimes feel in America as a minority, I will never fit in better elsewhere, even in Japan where I'm part of the racial majority.

When Mariko and I got back to the main room, the hanafuda cards were waiting for us. We played a game called *koi-koi*, which is a simple matching game. You pick up cards on the table by matching them to cards of the same suite in your hand. You try to get the highest-scoring cards, and simple design changes on the cards, like a colored ribbon as part of the design, indicate the value of cards. It's mostly luck, or at least that's what I told myself as Mariko wiped me out in short order. If I had won, then I would have opined that koi-koi is a game of skill, of course.

"Can I ask you something, Ken?" Mariko said as she leaned forward and scooped up the winnings from her latest hand. Her yukata was left open, revealing an expanse of skin and one breast. I don't know if this was through negligence or if it was a ploy to distract me from the game. If the latter, it was working.

"Ask me what?"

"Why are you doing this?"

"You mean playing cards? With the winning streak you're on, I'm asking that myself."

"No, I mean getting involved in another mystery. You were sort of pulled into the first mystery, but with this one you seem to be the one pursuing things. You've been running some awful risks with those guys after you. You think some people have been murdered for those swords, and yet you push on."

"I'm doing this because I don't have much going in my life, except for you. I'm over forty and unemployed and my life is half over. I don't want to play the second half as safe as I played the first half. This mystery has become important to me, and failing to solve it would be a kind of road block on the new path my life seems to be going down."

I said more than I intended, but I felt good about saying it. Mariko leaned over and kissed me on the cheek. It was a soft, gentle, loving kiss.

"Now," Mariko said, "even though we've had this tender moment that doesn't mean that I don't intend to take you for every penny you have. Dig into your pockets and produce the rest of your loose change. Japanese or American money cheerfully accepted. Shuffle the cards."

26

I could use a snack right now," Mariko said, placing down a hanafuda card.

"Since you've cleaned me out, I'll run into town and get something. There's no room service at the inn, or maybe I should say ryokan." I got off the zabuton cushion and stretched. "I'll be back in fifteen or twenty minutes."

"Don't get any of those dried fish or dried squid snacks," Mariko said. "Get us some real American potato chips or something like that."

"We're staying in a three-hundred-year-old Japanese inn and you want potato chips?"

Mariko looked at me and started going, "Yumm."

"I'll go, but you have to give me some money. You really have cleaned me out." She started laughing, but she did fork over several hundred-yen coins.

I took off the yukata I was wearing and got my jeans and a sweatshirt on. I pulled on my jacket and made my way through the corridors of the inn to the front lobby. The lobby was deserted, but I found my shoes sitting in the little numbered box right where I left them. I put them on and made my way down the little road towards the lights of the business district of town. The night air was brisk, and I sucked it in, relishing the relatively novel sensation of air not tainted with the smog of Los Angeles or Tokyo.

There was a certain amount of nightlife because the town was a resort center for people visiting Lake Biwa and the surrounding countryside. Although the main business district of town was only about four blocks long, there must have been a half-dozen bars stretched out along those blocks, with bright neon signs casting a splash of garish light onto the street.

I figured sooner or later I'd come to some kind of open convenience store or liquor store where they would have snacks to purchase. I wasn't quite sure about American-style potato chips, but I thought I could find something that would be good to munch on. There were a surprising number of people still milling around on the street at that time of night. Everybody seemed to be in a good mood, and even though the air was chilly, it was not so chilly that it was unpleasant.

I had walked about a half block into the business district when I stopped. At the end of the block, standing in front of a bar, was Junko. She had told us she wanted to take a shower and go to bed, so I was a bit surprised to see her out on the town. She was talking to a tall, thin man dressed in a topcoat with a hat pulled down low over his face. She seemed to be in earnest conversation when suddenly she looked up in alarm, grabbed the man by the arm, and quickly dragged him into the bar.

I looked across the street to see what had caused her to scurry into hiding with her companion. There, weaving through the crowd, was Sugimoto and another man who I didn't recognize. Both looked like they were drunk, staggering down the street together. Sugimoto had on his black leather jacket and his companion was dressed in jeans and a ski parka.

I turned quickly and hurried back up the hill to the ryokan. I was so excited that I almost forgot to take my shoes off when I got into the lobby. I remembered at the last minute before I tromped on the tatami mats, and stopped quickly to rip off my shoes and stuff them into one of the numbered boxes.

I made my way through the maze of corridors and burst into the room where Mariko was resting. She looked up in surprise.

"That was fast. What kind of snack did you buy?"

"I didn't buy any snacks. I saw something strange in town. Two things strange."

"What?"

"Sugimoto's in town. I saw him on the street in the village. He was there with another man. They looked like they were drunk."

"What's Sugimoto doing here?"

"Heaven knows. He's supposed to be in Osaka. Now I see him here with some stranger and I'm beginning to wonder about his role in this entire thing. I've been suspicious of him for some time now. He was able to arrange an interview with the head of the Sekiguchi-gummi pretty easily, and his family is supposed to be involved in the music business. The Yakuza are supposed to be involved in show business."

I unzipped my jacket and continued. "I also saw something else that's puzzling."

"What was that?"

"I saw Junko in town. She was talking to somebody I didn't recognize, someone tall with a hat on. The hat was pulled low so I couldn't see his face, as if he wanted to hide his identity."

"Did she see Sugimoto, too?"

"She sure did, and as soon as she saw him, she grabbed whoever she was with and ducked into a bar. She looked as startled to see Sugimoto as I did. I think she was trying to hide from him."

"That's strange. Maybe she just changed her mind about going to bed, got restless, and went into town and met someone."

"I bet she met someone," I said. "Maybe one of the guys who have been after me. One was a tall guy with a gold tooth. I didn't see his face, but the guy she was talking to was tall."

"Now you're getting paranoid."

"Am I? Geez, I never thought of this, but everybody's been telling me how many of the Yakuza members are Korean. One of the guys I identified was Korean. Junko's Korean."

"Ken, how many Italians do you know?"

I looked at Mariko, puzzled. "I suppose dozens, maybe even hundreds."

"And how many are members of the Mafia?"

"None that I know of."

"So why should Junko be a member of the Yakuza just

because she's Korean? You sound like some of the Japanese, classifying Junko as a criminal just because she's Korean."

"But there are Italians in the Mafia," I protested, "And there are Koreans in the Yakuza. She was up to something, and it was something that made her hide when she spotted Sugimoto. You're the one who's been having an uneasy time with her."

"That's just a little rivalry. But in this situation you're not sure what's going on."

"No, I'm not, but I don't like it. Sugimoto is supposed to be in Osaka. Junko lies to us about going to bed early. She hides when she sees Sugimoto. Something's fishy."

"Sugimoto is the one I'd worry about. He obviously followed us here. You said he's been against you investigating the swords from the beginning."

"That's right. Plus I don't know who Sugimoto's companion is. He might be another Yakuza, one I haven't seen yet."

"More Yakuza!"

"I have the bruises to remind me that someone is interested in me," I reminded her.

"I know. I'm sorry, Ken. It's just that first you think Junko is a Yakuza and now you think Sugimoto is one, too. That Sekiguchi-gummi head said he wasn't interested in you, and you thought it might be that political group."

"Maybe I was wrong. I just don't see the political connection. Sugimoto knew about my encounter with the two Yakuza in Tokyo, even though neither Junko nor I told him. He claims to be a rebel, but he longs for a return to values he considers 'true' Japanese, just like a lot of Yakuza. He's discouraged my investigation of the swords from the start. And now he shows up here unexpectedly and without telling us. All these things leave a lot of unanswered questions."

"Okay, so maybe Buzz Sugimoto is suspicious," Mariko conceded, "but saying Junko's a Yakuza is silly."

"Then who was she talking to, and why did she hide when she saw Sugimoto?"

"I don't know. Okay, okay, something fishy is going on. What do you think we should do about it? Confront Junko?" Mariko asked.

"No. In the morning, let's ask her how she slept and see what she says. If she says she got restless and went into town, then we should be upfront with her about me seeing her and ask her why Sugimoto's here. If she lies again, then I think we should be cautious."

"How?"

"Let's split up the search tomorrow. The center of the map is north of here, but let's tell Junko we should also search to the west of the town and that we'll split up to do it. We'll search the north and I'll find someplace in the west for her to search."

"Is that really necessary?"

I sighed. "You're the one who's been telling me I've gotten paranoid over the Yakuza thing. We can call the search off completely, but that will mean turning everything over to the *News Pop* show and Buzz or Junko can come up and look for the treasure after I leave Japan. Is that what you want?"

"No."

"Well, that doesn't leave us many choices, then. I could try going to the local police, but I don't have any proof of anything. I don't want to leave Japan without at least giving a shot at finding the treasure. And if Junko lies to us tomorrow, I don't want to have to worry about her at our back while Sugimoto may be in front of us. Do you have a better plan?"

After a few moments, Mariko said, "I hope Junko tells us in the morning that she couldn't sleep and went into the village where she picked up a guy. Then we can go treasure hunting together. Otherwise, I'll play along as you explain that you had a brainstorm about a new location for the treasure to the west."

T he forest was a wild and feral place. Giant cryptomerias grew in profusion. The rough, red bark of the trees clung to the large trunks, making a curtain that shrouded the forest beyond. Between the trees *hagi,* or bush clover, grew. A low morning mist clung to the roots of the trees, adding an eerie highlight to the forest.

"You sure you want to split up?" Junko asked.

"Yes. I was looking over the maps last night and I realized that the treasure was just as likely to be in the western part of the valley as here. It will be more efficient if you scout that location while Mariko and I look here. Meet us here at three o'clock and we'll compare notes. If we find anything interesting here, we'll still have time to take you to it so you can see what you want to film for the show."

That morning Junko had joined us claiming she had slept like a baby the night before. Mariko and I exchanged what Henry James used to call "significant looks." If I remember right, James meant those looks to signify love, but in our case the looks signified the cementing of a conspiracy to keep Junko away from the prime location for the treasure. I didn't know what was going on, but I did know we were being lied to.

"Okay, I'll see you at three this afternoon, then," Junko said as she put the Patrol in gear and pulled away.

"Are you ready?" I asked Mariko. She was bundled up and carrying a knapsack over one shoulder.

"Sure."

"Do you think we're doing the right thing?" I asked, a wave of second thoughts rolling over me.

She snorted her disdain for my backsliding and started purposefully down the path into the forest. Feeling a little foolish, I followed.

The hiking trail was well marked, so even though we plunged into a sort of gloomy twilight as we entered the forest, I didn't think we would get lost. I looked at Mariko and said, "So I gather you're ready to go treasure hunting?"

She stopped and let me catch up. She reached up and gave me a quick kiss on the lips. Her mouth was very cold and wet from the morning air. "I'm more than ready," she said. "Let's go see if we can find where there's a pile of gold."

"I don't see how we're going to find a group of trees or rocks that looks like an M," I said after we had been hiking for ten minutes or so. "I thought there'd be only a few groves of trees in this area, but now I see the whole area is a forest."

"Well, it's pretty anyway," Mariko said. "If we can't find billions in gold and silver, we can at least have a nice hike."

"That's very philosophical of you. I hoped to make enough off this treasure hunt to buy most of Japan. Now, according to you, I should just come back with a few memories of pretty countryside."

"You don't really expect to find the treasure, do you?"

"Well, I guess not," I admitted. "And if I did find it, I'm sure the government of Japan will have something to say about who keeps it. I haven't even checked into what the laws are about treasure hunting in Japan, but I'm sure it's not just finders-keepers."

We came across a stream that I had seen on the map and started following it. Despite my disappointment in seeing that the terrain was all woods, I was pretty happy. Having Mariko with me on this treasure hunt in Japan was an unexpected bonus, and it's always better when you share an exciting experience with someone you love. In the back of my mind, I just kept hoping that it wouldn't get too exciting, thanks to Sugimoto, Junko, the

Yakuza, the Nippon Tokkotai, and whoever else might be interested.

After hiking for about an hour, Mariko said, "I'm hungry."

"What? Already? It's not even ten o'clock."

"So what. Come on, let's stop and eat."

"I don't understand how someone as small as you can pack in so much food."

"Jealous?"

"Damn right. If I ate as much food as you, you'd have to roll me along the side of this stream because I'd be shaped like a barrel."

Mariko laughed and said, "Look, there's a little clearing ahead. Let's eat there. Mrs. Sakurai packed us some kind of lunch." She patted her knapsack. "And I'm anxious to see what kind of goodies we have. We'll have a picnic."

The clearing was like a miniature meadow by the side of the stream. Perhaps it was the aftermath of a long forgotten small fire, or perhaps the boulders that dotted the meadow gave a clue to the possibility that the ground was too rocky for the large trees to grow. Regardless, it let some sunlight into the gloom of the forest.

Mariko and I found a large rock to sit on. She unslung the pack, and before she got the lunches out, I leaned over and gave her a kiss. She gave me a happy hug in return. From the knapsack she brought out two black lacquered lunchboxes. She gave me one and took the top off the other and peered inside.

Inside was a pair of disposable chopsticks sitting on top of the beautifully prepared and neatly packed food. Rolls of rice covered with black sesame seeds and garnished with green, purple, and yellow pickles, made up one side of the box. Grilled fish, vegetables, and what looked like a rolled egg omelet made up the other half of the box. "Hey, that looks pretty good," I said, as I took the lid off my own *bento,* or box lunch. The Japanese would call this a honeymoon bento, because it was the kind of special lunch that a newly married salaryman could expect, prepared with care and with a delicious variety of foods. According to Japanese lore, eventually the salaryman would make the transition to a one–thousand Yen Samurai, whose wife would give him a daily allowance of one thousand yen with which he was supposed to buy lunch and other daily incidentals. In samurai times, the women kept the household purse strings, and many Japanese couples retain this custom, so a daily allowance for the man isn't unusual.

By the time I had my chopsticks broken apart, Mariko already had one of the rice rolls stuffed into her mouth. She closed her eyes in ecstasy and said, "Um. Delicious."

I tasted one of the rice rolls. "It's good."

"It's especially good. Maybe it's the way it's cooked, or maybe because they use spring water to cook it in."

"You don't think the fact that we're eating outdoors has anything to do with the way it tastes to you? Eating outdoors usually makes food taste better."

"Skeptic," she said. "Just eat your bento and don't bother me with your doubts. When I tell you it's delicious, it's because it's delicious. We could be eating inside a trailer parked in Kansas, and this rice would still be delicious."

I smiled and ate another rice roll.

Around us the brush and trees were still a bit lifeless, as if they were anticipating the impending winter, but I could tell that in the spring and early fall this area must be spectacular. I picked up a bit of the grilled fish and tasted it. It was very good. It had a charcoal flavor from being cooked over a hibachi. I picked up a piece of vegetable and looked up the mountainside that was on the other side of the stream as I brought it to my mouth.

I froze. Then I dropped the vegetable into my lap. Seeing the expression on my face, Mariko said, "What's the matter?"

Using the chopsticks, I pointed up the mountainside. "Look."

Mariko looked across the stream. On the other side she saw the rising slope of a wooded hill that rapidly turned itself into a mountain. At the top of the hill, sitting like some brooding castle, was an outcropping of rock. Two peaks of dark gray granite, forming the shape of the letter M.

"It's the pattern on the third blade," she said.

"That's right. It's an outcropping of rock."

I put the lunchbox down and stood up. Then I started dancing around the clearing. "We found it! We found it!" I grabbed the stunned Mariko by the hand and dragged her to her feet. "I'm sure that's it. We're gonna be rich. We're gonna be rich," I sang an improvised tune, dancing around Mariko. Okay, the lyrics weren't exactly Cole Porter, and I admit the tune wasn't Gershwin, but it sounded pretty damn good to me at the time.

A sharp crack rang out in the meadow and something hit the rock next to Mariko, scattering chips of stone and dirt. I pulled Mariko to the ground. "What was that?" she asked, startled.

I had a flashback to Vietnam. I was there only three weeks, but I knew exactly what was going on. "Somebody's shooting at us. Come on," I said. "Get behind the rock and let's get into the brush."

Mariko nodded and scuttled around the rock on her hands and knees. I followed. As we made our way into the brush, I heard excited voices from the other side of the clearing. "Get up and run like hell," I said. "Those guys mean business."

Mariko nimbly got to her feet and started running through the brush and trees with me crashing around behind her. As we ran I could hear shouts and voices behind us. "I think they're following us," I told Mariko.

I could see the forest ahead was getting thicker with brush and I realized that if we kept running in this direction we'd soon get tangled up and caught. "I'll cut to the left and cross the stream, making a lot of noise," I said. "You go ahead for a little bit, then cut to the right and double back towards where Junko dropped us off. Get help."

"No. I'm not going to leave you," Mariko said.

"Get back to the road and get help. I'm not acting like a hero, I'm just doing what's sensible. When I cut to the left, you go ahead and then double back. Find someone and get the police. Then bring them back here. If I lose them, I'll be hiding around the meadow. Okay?" I panted out the last few words. The thin mountain air made me tired, even after the short sprint.

"But Ken . . ."

"For God's sake, please do it! We've got to work together. We don't have time to argue."

"Okay." Mariko stopped running, turned around, and grabbed me around the neck. With my forward momentum, it almost tumbled us to the ground. She gave me a brief, fierce kiss and said, "I love you. I'll bring back help, no matter what. Don't take any risks!"

"Don't be silly. Just get help. I love you, too." She let go of my neck and started running to the right, up the slope of a hill. My grand plan was for her to go forward a little before she cut to the right, but the way she darted through the woods like a deer made me think she probably knew more about it than I did. Now my job was to draw off our pursuers. I turned left and started crashing through the brush, shouting to an imaginary companion. I could hear people yelling to each other, so I was sure they could hear me, too.

I came the edge of the stream. It was only four feet wide and I jumped it at a dead run. Now I was running uphill and fatigue started dragging at my legs. Behind me I heard shouting, so I knew I was being followed. I also knew I couldn't elude my pursuers long enough for Mariko to get help unless I thought of something more imaginative than just staying ahead of them.

As I clambered higher up the hill the slope got steeper and the thick trunks of the trees grew closer together. Below me I could hear men shouting to each other. It sounded like three of them, and they had spread out into a picket line, making inexorable progress up the mountainside. I realized I would soon be trapped.

I looked around for a weapon and, acting on an instinct as old as man, I stooped down and picked up a rock the size of my fist. Then I looked for a place to hide.

Ahead I saw two trees growing so closely together that the trunks of the trees were mated, forming an expanse of wood wide enough for me to hide behind. I scurried up the slope and got to the uphill side of the trees. Then I pressed back against the trunks, pushing my back against the unyielding wood and holding the rock tightly in my hand.

My breath came in ragged gasps and my heart was beating so loudly I was sure the men would be able to hear it long before they came upon the tree. I fought to control my breathing, closing my eyes momentarily and trying to focus my energy.

Around me the woods took on a strange silence and time seemed to pass with excruciating slowness. I was sure they were right behind me, but I stood pressed against the trees so long that I thought they might have given up the chase.

Then I heard the slide of rocks and dirt as someone scrambled up the hillside. The sound came closer and I raised the rock. If the man passed more than a few feet away, I realized I was probably a dead man because there was no way to throw the rock faster than the flight of a bullet. Besides, as a kid, baseball was not my game. I wasn't sure how good my aim was.

My lungs were burning and I realized I had been holding my breath. I allowed myself the luxury of a slow exhale as I waited for the first sign of my pursuers.

Suddenly, at the edge of the tree, a brown hand grasped the trunk. On instinct, I stepped from behind the tree and brought the rock down with all my weight behind it. The wolfish Yakuza looked up with surprise. In his other hand was a gun, but he was off balance, pulling himself up the hillside, and couldn't get a shot off.

The rock came crashing down on his cheekbone with a sickening crunch. He crumpled, releasing the gun and letting it skitter down the steep hillside. I fought to regain my balance so I wouldn't go tumbling down the slope, too.

I grabbed the tree to steady myself and looked down at the man. Fresh blood already covered one side of his face, and he was making a feeble attempt to cover his head with his arms. The smart thing to do would have been to hit him again to finish him off, but I guess I'm not smart. I didn't feel remorse for hitting him. The bastard had a gun and, for all I knew, he was the one who had shot at Mariko and me. But I just didn't have the stomach to strike a second blow.

Instead, I looked for the gun that had slipped down the slope. I couldn't see it, and I was about to start a search for it when I heard another voice shouting to my right. The voice called a couple of times, and I heard the man at my feet moan a kind of response. I figured someone would be coming to investigate why their buddy wasn't responding to their hail, and it was time to move out again.

Abandoning my search for the gun, I dropped the rock and started scrambling up the hill again.

28

I made my way farther up the mountainside and hid in the forest. Whenever I stopped to listen for the sounds of pursuit I heard nothing but an eerie stillness and the sound of a light breeze rustling the tree branches. I started thinking about making my way back towards the meadow when I realized I was on the side of the stream with the rocks shaped like the letter **M** and already up the steep slope where the rocks perched.

I decided to check out the rocks. I wasn't motivated by greed. By this time, thoughts of actually keeping any treasure were the furthest thing from my mind. I was motivated by an intense curiosity and a desire to see things to their conclusion. I know what curiosity did to the cat, but I wasn't a cat. I hoped.

I cut to my left and started making my way through the forest. After twenty minutes or so, I came out of the trees and I was confronted by the outcropping of rocks, which appeared very much like a castle close up. I looked around carefully to make sure that none of my pursuers were near, then slowly approached the rocks.

When I got up to the rocks, I realized there was a kind of seam in their face, a fissure that led back into the rock. I peered down the fissure and saw what looked like the entrance to a cave. Taking one last look around to make sure I was alone, I walked into the fissure and what lay beyond.

As I approached the cave entrance I was able to see that it was overgrown with brush. I don't know if this was how it was almost four hundred years ago when the treasure was placed here, but now it was a perfect hiding place because it was almost totally invisible until you were right on it. I peered into the cave, down a natural tunnel that was six to seven feet high at the entrance. The sunlight did not penetrate into the depths.

I entered and felt something crunching under my feet. I looked down and saw some bleached animal bones. Fortunately, they were all small bones and none were big enough to be human. At least that's what I told myself. Over the years, some wild animal had evidently used the cave as a den. I hoped whatever animal was involved wasn't currently in residence.

I stopped for a few moments to let my eyes get used to the darkness, but it wasn't much use. The light from the entrance was swallowed up about fifteen feet down the tunnel. I didn't have a flashlight, but I wasn't about to let something like good sense stop me. I felt I was close to the treasure and the allure of gold easily pierced the darkness in front of me. Blind, I plunged deeper into the cave, out of the half light of the entrance and into the black.

I moved in short shuffling steps, holding my hands above me at head height to make sure I didn't bump into a low ceiling. As I got into the cave, the air was damp and heavy and the velvet darkness soon swallowed up any remaining visibility. I had no feeling for how large or small the cave might be. I thought it would be a good strategy to get to one wall and brush my hands against it.

Before I could do that I bumped into something. It startled me because although behind me I could still dimly see the light from the entrance, in front of me it was pitch black. I stopped and reached down. Instead of feeling a solid object, something crumbled under my hand. I felt like I was plunging my hand into a large mound of dry leaves. I couldn't figure out what it was. It was weird and unsettling.

"You know," I said out loud, "this is the final dumb thing you've done on a pretty dumb day." I turned around and groped towards the light of the cave entrance. I didn't know what I had encountered, but I did know I didn't like it.

As I walked out of the cave, before my eyes could adjust from the gloom and darkness of the interior to the sunlight, a blow struck me across the shoulder and base of my neck. Stumbling with pain and surprise, I fell to one knee, grabbing at my shoulder. I looked up and saw Professor Hirota advancing towards me. He had somehow appeared behind me at the cave's entrance. In Hirota's hands, held before him like an ancient samurai sword, was a tree branch.

I scrambled to my feet and took a step backwards before the advancing tip of the tree limb could strike another blow. I was trapped in the narrow fissure that led to the cave entrance and couldn't move to the right or left, only backwards.

Hirota did not smile. His face was set in rigid lines, his eyes watching every move I made. "Are you surprised to see me?" he asked.

"A little, but I figured you knew more than you were telling when you sent me off to Kyoto to meet with Sonoda-san instead of just telling me the legend. It was also strange that Sonoda-san's blade wasn't stolen, which could mean either you or Sonoda-san were involved. Besides, you didn't have the hands of a scholar. Most Japanese wouldn't notice because they bow, but a Western handshake can tell you a lot." Actually, I wasn't that clever. With him standing before me, a lot of things clicked into place, but the truth was that I was very surprised to see him. However, when you're shocked, hurt, and scared spitless, a little stupid macho posturing is allowed. It comes from watching too many Humphrey Bogart movies. "Where did you come from?" I asked.

"From nowhere. I am the shadow. I am the wind. The way of Ninjitsu teaches me to be invisible."

"Ninjitsu?"

"The way of the Ninja," Hirota said. "I was quite invisible and you walked right past me."

I didn't believe him. It was his turn to do some macho posturing. It's a male thing. My eyes darted past him and I searched for where he had been hiding. I couldn't see a place in the narrow confines of the fissure. Maybe he was invisible. He saw my eyes looking around and he smiled. It was a smile that brought me no comfort.

"I see you don't believe me," Hirota said. "In that case, I don't suppose you would believe that a Ninja can see into your heart and that I knew you were coming here."

I looked at him warily, but made no reply. Considering our relative positions, I thought it was best to curb my tongue.

"You spotted this place when you and the girl were eating down by the river bank," Hirota continued. "My companions decided it was time to remove you from the picture. They can be a bunch of asses at times, but you have been a bloody irritant to us. In fact, in a way, you are the cause of all this."

"Me?"

"Yes. I saw your picture in the *Asahi Shimbun* and realized you were holding a Toyotomi blade. I've tracked the locations of the blades for years. Your photograph showed me the blade that I needed most of all, and it spurred me to action."

I looked behind me at the forest. I wondered what my chances were of getting back into the safety of the woods.

Hirota saw me glancing towards the shelter of the trees. "I wouldn't plan on it," he said. "The back of your head would make a tempting target if you started to run away from me. I'm not sure how fast you can run, but it would be an interesting game to see if I could catch you." He smiled. "Besides, I have a gun in my pocket."

Then I wondered if I could stall Hirota until Mariko arrived with the police. As if reading my mind, Hirota added, "I'll make the decision what to do with you long before your girlfriend has a chance to get back with the police. It will take them quite a while to get here. Japanese police are not paragons of efficiency."

Hirota took a quick step forward and I jumped back. Hirota laughed, enjoying the game. "Do you know that at times students are killed with wooden *kendō* swords? The swords have lead in them to approximate the heft and feel of a real sword and in the heat of a match students sometimes get carried away and there are serious injuries or even death. This tree limb—" Hirota lifted the tip of the limb slightly—"does not have the same feel as a sword, but I can still make it do almost anything I wish. For instance, I could quite easily shatter your kneecap or poke out an eye."

He made no move to put either threat into action, so I said,

"Why would you want to do that?" I wanted it to sound nonchalant, but I'm afraid it came out with a bit of a quaver.

"Because right now I am cross and feel cheated. More important, you are part of the reason I was cheated."

I decided to try and change the subject. "You said I had the blade you wanted most of all, but that was only five of them. One's still missing."

"I have the missing sixth blade. It's been in my family for generations. We've always been taught to hide the fact, and unlike Sonoda-san's family, we have. It's foolish, I know, because the Toyotomi are never coming back. Still, if a family can be loyal to a certain brand of automobile, buying nothing but that brand across generations, I guess my family's loyalty to the responsibilities they accepted along with the sword isn't too peculiar."

"And you stole the blade in New York? The police said they thought someone was lowered from the roof."

He sneered. "The police everywhere have no imagination. Ninja have tools used to scale steep castle walls. They work amazingly well on a modern skyscraper."

"And the man killed in the robbery?"

Hirota smiled again. "Why would I admit to doing that?"

That gave me my first hope that I might get out of this alive. He wouldn't be cautious if he thought I wouldn't be around to testify against him.

"I will tell you one thing," Hirota continued.

"What's that?"

"Studying to kill a man and actually killing one are two very different things."

I was going to pursue this interesting statement, but decided discretion really is the better part of valor. Instead, I asked, "What about the Rotterdam blade?"

Hirota laughed. "That was trivial. All it took was a piece of string, a wire, and the ability to blend into a group of Japanese tourists. If you think about it, I'm sure someone as clever as you will be able to figure that one out."

"And the student who was accused of stealing the sword from the Japanese National Museum?"

The smile was wiped from Hirota's face. Bad move on my part.

"I was in Los Angeles trying to steal your sword from your flat when the student, Ishibashi, died."

"The burglar that Mrs. Hernandez saw!"

"Is that the old woman who lives above your flat?"

"Yes."

"She caused me a little difficulty. I had to cut short my search of your flat when the police showed up, but I would have returned the next night to finish the job. Instead I had an excited message from my colleagues that you were in Japan with the sword and would be appearing on a television show." The TV promo. "I told them to follow you to see what hotel you were staying at while I arranged a flight back to Japan. Unfortunately, their enthusiasm exceeded their ability to perform even that simple task, and they decided to catch you and force you to give them the sword. Fools. When I got back to Japan and found out that the TV show was trying to contact me about the blades, I was ecstatic. When you actually gave me your blade to examine, I thanked the gods."

"So you were in Los Angeles when the student died?"

"Yes. Ishibashi was a student of mine. He was going to Waseda, but also taking a class in Japanese history from me at All Japan University. He took the sword from the Japan National Museum to please me. I would not have hurt him."

"So it was actually a suicide?"

Hirota looked at me a long minute. Then he said, "The members of a group like the Nippon Tokkotai may be filled with Yamato Damashii, but they aren't always filled with good judgment. They thought the proper way to insure silence in Ishibashi was to eliminate him. If I was in Japan, I would not have allowed it."

"Who did it?"

Another pause. Then Hirota said, "You took care of Mr. Kim very smartly with a rock. It knocked the treasure hunting zeal out of him."

"So Kim killed the student?"

Hirota smiled. "Even the Japanese police might come to the

truth of things if they stopped accepting any plausible explanation and sought the facts."

"I'll take that as a yes."

Hirota shrugged. "Have you had a chance to inspect the treasures that our long search has brought us?"

"It was too dark for me," I admitted. "I couldn't tell what was in there. I bumped into something that felt weird, but other than that . . ." I let the sentence trail away. I kept my eyes on the tree limb Hirota held in front of him.

"After I explored the treasures in the cave, I was thoroughly disgusted. I told my companions and they wanted to leave immediately. Especially Mr. Kim. But I came back alone to see if there was something I had missed. I saw you just as you entered the cave. I picked up a branch and waited for you because I wanted to know your reaction to the treasure in the cave."

"I didn't have a flashlight. I couldn't see what's in the cave."

Hirota laughed. "The master detective and you forgot to bring a flashlight. Amazing."

"What's in the cave?" I asked.

"Bails of rotting silk and rotting brocades. That's all that's in the cave. We looked it over quite carefully. There's no gold and there's no silver, just rotting clothes left to turn to dust after hundreds of years of decay. It was quite a disappointment. We had plans for the money we assumed would be there."

"Could the gold or silver be buried someplace in the cave?"

"The floor and walls are solid rock. Thanks to your meddling, I won't have a chance to find out for sure, but I think that the gold and silver are gone. Assuming they were ever in there, someone must have found them and took them. For some reason, they left all the brocade and silk clothes. Maybe when the treasure was found, they were already rotting. You know, it took me a long time to match the map found on the blades to the right area of Japan. I don't see how it was possible for you to put together a map without all six of the blades."

"We used a computer. We matched the patterns on the five blades we had to a computerized map of Japan. That's how I ended up here."

Hirota shook his head. "All this high technology is the ruin of Japan. It's made us forget our traditions and heritage. Soon we'll be just a pale imitation of the United States." I figured if I could keep him talking I could play for time. As Hirota talked, the blade dipped downwards in very slow increments.

"Everybody wants to preserve their culture," I said. "But you know Japan can never go back. For better or worse, it's wedded to the West. That wedding has brought a lot of benefits."

"It's also had a great price: the restructuring of our national identity."

"But your culture was changing anyway. Even before the war, Japanese culture was not like the culture of the people who left that treasure in there. Three hundred years of social evolution saw to that. You can't go back."

"But we want to go back. We yearn to go back. With the help of groups like the Nippon Tokkotai, we will go back. It's simply a matter of gathering enough money to further our program."

"Is that what this is all about? Money?" I asked.

"With the bursting of our bubble economy, the funding for the Nippon Tokkotai has dried up," Hirota said. "Japanese politics is fueled by money, much like the politics in your own country. The organization saw this as a way of raising large amounts of cash to finance activities. We need that cash to become a force in national politics in Japan, to return us to the values we've forgotten since our defeat in the Pacific War. We needed that treasure, and now it's gone."

"The treasure would have been gone whether I got involved or not."

Hirota nodded. "I suppose so. A very logical observation. I think that's what's wrong with all of us now. At least us Japanese."

"What do you mean?"

"We've become too logical. Despite what you Westerners think, we Japanese have always been a very emotional people. We cry at poems and think suicide can be beautiful. In the ancient days, the samurai would follow duty and emotion and not logic. We still tend to do that sometimes, but more and more we Japanese are becoming rational creatures of the Western world." Hirota's tree limb was now pointing towards the ground. "Three hundred years ago, I'd have killed you just for revenge and then killed myself for failing."

"But it's not three hundred years ago."

"True. More's the pity. I'm sure my friends from the Nippon Tokkotai have already left. In a remote location like this, it's going to be easy enough for the police to radio ahead and set up a roadblock, once your girlfriend gets to them. I still have to decide what I'm going to do with myself." He paused. "And with you."

"Do you remember the end to Kurosawa's film *Hidden Fortress*?" I asked.

He looked at me like I had lost my mind, asking a question about an old samurai movie. Then he understood my point and laughed. "You mean the part where the bad guy captures Toshiro Mifune, but lets him go because that's the honorable thing to do?"

Bingo. "That's the part exactly. That movie reflects the Japan you say you love. It recognizes that *bushido*, the way of the warrior, involves honor and chivalry. Any rivalry between us had nothing to do with you and me personally. I didn't know who I was competing with to find the treasure, and frankly you weren't at the top of my list. Our rivalry was over finding that." I nodded towards the treasure cave. "You had the six blades and I had the technology that you say is ruining Japan. We both got here at the same time. I'd prefer a clear win for technology because that would mean that you wouldn't be standing here in front of me, but if I get out of this, I'll be satisfied with a draw.

"Despite your talk of suicide, I think you want to live. It's occurred to me that it will be a lot easier for you to live if I live, too. The *News Pop* television show is going to do a special about the blades in a few days, and if you kill me, that special will be all about me. Not because they love me at *News Pop*, but because it will mean terrific ratings for them. The death of some Mafia Don in New York isn't a big story in Japan, but killing me while I'm investigating something for *News Pop* will be big news here. If they capture your companions from the Nippon Tokkotai, as you think they will, even the Japanese police will eventually figure out your involvement. With the pressure from television if I die, it will be a lot harder for you to get away."

"So I'm supposed to just release you?"

"It's what happened in *Hidden Fortress*."

Hirota laughed. He shook his head. "I must be a fool, letting you talk me into something based on an old samurai movie." He dropped the tree limb. If Akira Kurosawa, the director of *Hidden Fortress,* had been there, I'd have kissed him.

"What are you going to do?" I asked.

"There's a Japanese tradition of defeated leaders and bandits taking to the mountains. I'm going to see that particular tradition doesn't die. It's been an interesting experience meeting you, and some day, assuming we ever see each other again, you're going to have explain to me all the computer magic you used to find this place."

Hirota walked past me, moving rapidly towards the forest.

"Hirota!" I shouted just before he entered the woods. He turned to look at me, puzzled. "You were above the entrance of the cave and dropped down on me, hitting me as you hit the ground. That's why I didn't see you when I came out of the cave."

He grinned. "You're too damn smart. You'll take the mystery out of life, if you don't watch it. Then it won't be fun."

Rubbing my shoulder, I stood watching while he disappeared into the woods.

The brightness of the lights, the ordered confusion of the crew, and the small confines of the *News Pop* studio were beginning to feel familiar to me. For the last couple of days *News Pop* had been on an advertising blitz, hyping the show and the discovery of the Toyotomi treasure. The show had gotten considerable press coverage in the Japanese media. So had I.

Mariko and I had been on sightseeing trips to Asakusa, Yokohama, and Kamakura, courtesy of *News Pop,* and some people recognized me on the street. A few of the braver English-speaking souls even came up and asked me if I was the Sansei detective, and after the first couple of times, I got tired of explaining I wasn't a detective and I simply said yes. I even signed a couple of autographs! In Los Angeles, I'm a total nobody. Here in Tokyo, the TV show was making me a minor celebrity. It was a weird metamorphosis, made stranger because it happened in just a few days.

Mariko and I were both going to be on the show. The length of the show was extended another thirty minutes as a special on the discovery of the Toyotomi treasure. Because of the composition of that "treasure," I learned one thing about fame. It doesn't necessarily mean fortune. Museum experts were talking about trying to restore some of the clothes to put on display, but that restoration process was actually going to cost somebody a lot of money. A treasure that takes money out of people's pockets is not the kind of treasure that makes its discoverer wealthy.

On the night of the show, the lady who did the makeup for the show finished and left the makeup room. Mariko glanced out the door to make sure she was gone, then hurriedly picked up some blusher and an eyebrow pencil and changed the line of her eyebrows slightly and added a few more highlights to her cheeks. She took a sponge and blended it expertly so that the highlights looked natural. As an actress, she was used to doing her own makeup and she knew the difference between TV makeup, stage makeup, and the kind of makeup people commonly wear every day. I have to say that her little touches did make a definite improvement.

I suppose a real hard-boiled detective at this point would have made some crack about dames always having to look good on camera, but seeing the improvement that Mariko made, I asked her to adjust my makeup, too. She smiled, and with a few quick expert swipes with a sponge and the use of a couple of bottles on the makeup table, she had me looking my best, too.

She finished just in time. As she put the sponge down on the table, Sugimoto appeared at the door to take us to the greenroom. I walked next to Sugimoto and said, "Can I ask you something?"

"What?"

"After the thugs hit me in the park, you knew about it even though Junko didn't tell you. How?"

Sugimoto looked puzzled and said, "The producers called me in and yelled at me about it. After Junko told them about the incident and your need to get out of Tokyo, they said it was my responsibility and that I should have walked you back to the hotel or taken you there in a cab. That's how I knew what was going on."

"And why did you appear at the village, even though you were supposed to be scouting out the other location in Osaka?"

"I went to Osaka and found out that the center of the map is a housing tract. Even if the treasure had been there, I don't know how we could have dug up peoples' houses trying to find it. And to be honest with you, I knew that you had gone with Junko up to the Lake Biwa location. Junko and I have a sort of rivalry going because we both have good language skills and we're often going after the same kinds of stories. I thought she was trying to do some sneaky trick on me by taking the Lake Biwa site and taking you with her. I decided to tag along and bring a cameraman, too. What I suspected was true and the scouting trip turned into a treasure hunt. I was glad I was there with the cameraman to capture the police action in the mountains after Professor Hirota left you. That's got to be some of the most exciting footage on tonight's show. Not to mention the footage we shot with lights inside the cave where the treasure was."

Sugimoto deposited us in the greenroom. Mr. Sonoda was there from Kyoto and he greeted us warmly. We had already had a conversation earlier that evening, but he still greeted me with the enthusiasm usually reserved for an old friend. I appreciated it. There was also some professor from Tokyo University who was an expert in restoring textiles. Unfortunately, the professor didn't speak English, although Mr. Sonoda translated as the professor thanked me profusely for providing him with a treasure trove of clothes.

Sonoda-san said the professor thought it would take ten or fifteen years to restore all the clothes found in the cave. I suppose that if the professor was good at his work some day the contents of the cave really would be a treasure, in terms of a glimpse into the courtly clothes of the early seventeenth century.

When they took Mr. Sonoda and the professor to the set, Junko joined us in the greenroom and gave us a running translation for the show. She didn't do that the first time I was on the show, and I was amused to see that even she was giving us the VIP treatment.

They opened the show with an interview with Sonoda-san, where he repeated the story of the Toyotomi blades to set the historical scene of what was to follow. He speculated that the treasure might have been stolen in ancient times, maybe even by the Tokugawas, who could have used the money to defeat the Toyotomis who hid it. He explained that in ancient times, expensive clothing was very valuable, and it was often a favorite gift bestowed by a lord to a vassal. All the clothes in the cave were unique, valuable pieces that, four hundred years ago, would have been as precious as gold or silver. He said this would explain why the clothes were left in the cave even if the gold had been stolen in ancient times. It would be too easy to identify the clothes because they all had distinctive patterns, and this would tip off the Toyotomi that the treasure was gone.

Then they showed a film piece made up of the footage Sugimoto shot around the cave and in the mountains. It showed how wild and rugged the location was. The footage inside the cave showed several gray-colored bales of cloth sitting on the cave floor, rotting away.

After the film clip, they interviewed the professor from Tokyo University. He had some still shots of some of the clothes he was working on initially. They looked dirty and brown and rotted away, but he assured the audience that he would be able to restore many of them to their former glory. To prove it, he showed some pieces of cloth he had restored and the colors were nice and vibrant. The professor seemed extremely excited about all the garments that he would have to examine over the upcoming years.

They cut to commercial and Junko left to prepare for translating for Mariko. After she left I said to Mariko, "You and Junko seem to have called a truce."

"As we were preparing for this show, we had a chance to talk."

"About what?"

"None of your business."

"Come on, that's not fair."

"She was talking about how hard it is to be a woman in Japan, especially if you're part of a minority. I can relate to that, being raised in Columbus, Ohio. I told her we knew she met someone at the village."

"You told her that?"

"Yes. She was shocked. She didn't know if you're really some kind of master detective or just a plain snoop. I told her you were just a guy buying potato chips in a town too small to hide anything."

"Who's the man?"

"He's the technical director on the show. They're having an affair."

"Why did she hide him?"

She sighed. "He's married. It's hard for a Korean to have a relationship in Japan, even if she wants to hide the fact she's a Korean. A Japanese will check your family history, and if he sees you're a Korean, he or his family will probably discriminate against you. She claims he wants to get a divorce from his wife, but he hasn't yet. He met her at Lake Biwa because they could spend a night together. His wife was off visiting relatives. She didn't want Sugimoto to see them because she thought Sugimoto was there to poach on the story and didn't want to give him any ammunition by revealing she's having an affair with a married man. That's why she hid and that's why she didn't mention Sugimoto to us the next morning. I feel sorry for her. This guy is probably handing her a line about leaving his wife and she'll end up as just another sad story about a single girl seeing a married man."

I was sorry, too. Not because of the probable fate of Junko's love affair, but because I found myself just as prejudiced as the Japanese majority. I thought she had a Yakuza connection because she was Korean. It was stupid. I get outraged when I encounter this type of thinking back in the States, especially when it's directed at Asians, but as soon as I found myself in the majority, I slipped into the ready comfort of a stereotypical prejudice. It was a sobering lesson, and one I'm not proud to admit to.

An aide came to get Mariko, and Sugimoto joined me in the greenroom to translate. I realized it was the show's producers who probably ordered the VIP treatment for me, not something Junko had done on her own. After a few commercials for some kind of vitamin drink, they started showing a piece about the Nippon Tokkotai. It discussed their past involvement in radical, right-wing causes that were designed to return Japan to a militaristic country. It also showed a red-faced spokesman for the group denying any knowledge of the efforts to use the treasure to further their political agenda.

Then the show ran clips from news shows that showed the capture of Kim and his companion, Honda. As Hirota had predicted, the police were able to set up a roadblock and an amateur video cameraman happened to be on hand to get footage of a bloody Kim being pulled from a car. They ran a second clip of a serious police spokesman announcing that Kim had confessed to the murder of Ishibashi, the student. Unlike the Matsumoto case, I have no doubts that this confession is true. I do have suspicions about how the Japanese police were able to obtain a confession so quickly, though.

They showed some film of the Japanese police combing the mountains by Lake Biwa. Having seen Hirota's ability to disappear into the forest, I wasn't surprised the Japanese police couldn't catch him on foot. I was surprised that even bringing in helicopters to help search the area didn't unearth a clue about where Hirota had gone, however. It was as if he had turned himself invisible.

Watching the piece, I wondered about Hirota and where he was at that moment. I was curious if he was still in the mountains, hiding someplace and living off the land. Or perhaps he had already found his way back to civilization and had started blending into society. If I was Javert, Hirota's escape would bother me. But, unlike the fictional detective in Victor Hugo's classic, I felt no need to pursue him until every last demand of the law was settled. I figured the books between us were balanced and closed. Maybe Sonoda-san was right and my view of the law is more Confucian than Western.

Then it was Mariko's turn. She did great. Her stage training really showed. In fact, Nagahara-san and Yukiko-chan commented on what wonderful presence she had on camera. I could see that pleased Mariko, and it pleased me, too. Then more commercials and it was finally my turn. The grand finale.

They rushed me into my seat and fitted me with the earphone so that I could hear the translation. When they got back from commercial, they introduced me and they immediately went to a clip that showed me entering the Nissan building and working with Kiyohara-san and the rest of the Nissan crew to develop the computerized maps we used to find the treasure. After the clip they cut back to me and the interview. Nagahara-san and Yukiko-chan started peppering me with questions about how I solved the mystery, what happened when they were shooting at us in the forest, and what Hirota said to me during our final confrontation.

Before going on camera, I had sworn that I would try to be suitably modest. After the events of the last few days, I figured that I would have to carry my head onto the plane resting in a wheelbarrow if I didn't watch it. By acting modestly in the interview, a strange thing happened. The more modest I became, the more effusive the two anchors were with their praise. It was as if my modesty gave them permission to lay it on thick when they talked about me and what had been accomplished. It was a valuable lesson and one that taught me the old adage about less is more.

During a lull in the conversation, Junko whispered to me through my earpiece, "Keep it up, the producers are loving it."

As the show came to a close, Nagahara-san said to me, "So what are your future plans?"

That was a good question, and one I hadn't planned for. Most of the questions were about the mystery, and I had either been told or could anticipate what they were. This gave me a chance to work out some reasonably cogent answers. This was one I hadn't thought of, so I just answered from the heart.

"Well, first I'll return to the United States. It's been a joy to come to Japan, and it's an experience that every Japanese-American should have. A part of me will always be Japanese because it's in my blood. But like most people in America, visiting the home of my ancestors has reminded me of the sacrifices my parents and grandparents made to make a new home in America, and I realize I am truly an American.

"Before the show I talked to Mr. Sonoda, and he made a very generous offer to buy my sword. I'm sure he's offering more than it's worth, but I'm going to take advantage of his generosity because the money will allow me to pursue something I've been toying with for a couple of months." Mariko was in the back of the studio watching my interview. She couldn't understand the question because she didn't have an earpiece for the translation, but she could understand my answer.

"When I get back to California, I'm going to investigate what it will take to make me a licensed private investigator. If I can qualify, I'm going to use Mr. Sonoda's money to pursue that goal." I glanced over at Mariko. She wasn't shaking her head yes, but she wasn't shaking her head no, either. That's a start.